W9-BSO-148

Chapter 1

While they talk about their upcoming trips to places like the Bahamas, I remember this is the last day that cheese is on sale. I pull a pen from my purse then write the word "cheese" on the palm of my hand so I won't forget.

Girls hang around in groups in the locker room as they stretch their legs, pull back their hair, and make small talk. Kennedy, a senior cheerleader, sees a plastic Maui souvenir keychain hanging from someone's bag and gets excited.

"Maui is the best, by far. The waves are huge and the tropical flowers everywhere make for great pictures. And basically the whole island smells like Bath and Body Works."

Another chimes in, "Yeah, I've been to Maui, but I still like the Keys best. The sand is softer. Whiter."

Cassidy makes eye contact with me. She knows I can't participate in this conversation.

Five of them, including Cassidy, compare sand textures and amenities of resorts I've never even heard of while I try to conceal my impromptu grocery list. Before someone can ask me about *my* favorite beach, I toss my bag in an unused locker then head out to the gym floor. Miss Mound sits in the bleachers and thumbs through paperwork. She looks up.

"Hey, Chelsea."

"Hi, Miss Mound." I sit down and go into the butterfly stretch. She goes back to organizing paperwork. Extending my legs in front of me, I reach for my toes then lie on my back and bend at the knees, cupping my hands behind my head. I stare into the rafters and think about beaches. The air. Is it different? The water. Is it cold? How does it feel to run your feet through sand? Do they really have little bar huts like they do in the movies?

Fifteen other girls make their way out into the gym. The conversation has switched to favorite ski resorts. I crisscross my legs, look down, and open my hand to stare at the word "cheese." Cassidy sits next to me and twists her thick, gorgeous, brown hair into a knot on the top of her head as Miss Mound turns on some hip-hop music to get things started.

"Girls, let's begin with kicks today." This is our cue to get up and get into formation, and that's exactly what we do. What am I doing here? And how will I be able to pull this off?

I stop by the store on the way home and buy a generic bag of tortilla chips to go with the cheese. This will get us through the week, Dad and me. I pull into our oil-stained driveway and shift my five speed into park. Grabbing my backpack and grocery bag, I head to check the mail. On my way to the mailbox, I bend down and pull a weed the size of a small tree that's been thriving in a cement crack for about a month now, and toss it on the lawn. I've been in charge of the mail for years, but each time I open the rusty lid, *screeeeech*, I get nervous about what may be inside. Because most of the time, along with pizza coupons, postcards, and miscellaneous junk, there are two little words in that stack somewhere: Amount Due.

It's not the first time. Probably not the last.

The infamous cut-off notice. There's the ten-day notice, then there's the forty-eight-hour notice. Fortunately, this one is the former so I've got ten days to get this figured out. I step inside the house and read the fine print in hopes for a loophole:

When the temperature is actually, or predicted to be, 101 degrees Fahrenheit heat index or higher on the day of disconnection or the nighttime low is predicted to be 20 degrees Fahrenheit or less, OG&E will suspend disconnection of service.

Unfortunately, we've had the most beautiful fall weather—low eighties—so this won't help us out.

Although this is about the millionth time we've received a cut-off notice, we've actually only been cut off twice. Once in junior high. Once in elementary school— fourth grade picture day, to be exact.

"Chelsea, did you forget it was picture day?" Ms. Foltz greeted me at the door. "Honey, your hair is dripping wet."

I hung my backpack on my hook. There was a plethora of

curls, plastic headbands, and outfits with iron creases around. But me? Wet hair.

Everyone, and I do mean everyone, looked like they stepped out of a television commercial. Picture order envelopes filled out by their moms pulled out of backpacks and folders, checks enclosed. Package A was the popular choice, they discovered, after everyone compared.

I tucked in my shirt then trudged to my desk. I tried several times to complete the first math problem for morning work, but I couldn't. Just couldn't. I walked back to the classroom door where Ms. Foltz continued to greet each student, complimenting them each on their adorable outfits and "gorgeous" hairdos.

"Ms. Foltz, may I use the restroom?"

"Sure, Chelsea," she responded, then looked over me to yet another adorable picture day kid. "Looook at you! All fancy-schmancy for picture day!"

Walking to the bathroom, I was practically blinded by all of the shiny curls. I went straight to the mirror and started combing my hair with my fingers, as fast as possible, to try to add some life to the limp mess. I squatted down under the hand drier, pushed the big round button, and started drying my hair. I restarted it seven times. Seven cycles of drying, scrunching, and fluffing . . .

I don't think Dad even knew it was picture day. I had forgotten to tell him.

Chapter 2

I brainstorm ways to get money to pay the electric bill. There's a little in my savings account, but Dad has always forbidden any withdrawals because the $100 that sits in there is earmarked "for college." He has good intentions. Honestly, he does. But I'm not sure how a $100 college fund can magically turn into thousands in one short year. I mean really. How?

It would take at least three weeks for me to receive a paycheck, and that's if I started a new job, like, *today*. I could donate my plasma . . . but how much would I even make? Robbing a bank is probably out of the question, and there's no chance of hitting the lottery when you're too young to play it. It takes me all of six steps to get from the front door to the back, where I drop my backpack and stare out the window. Patchy grass, weeds, and missing fence panels . . . but nope, still no money tree out there.

I walk into the living room and give Dad a little nudge on the couch to wake him up. "Dad, I'm home."

He opens his eyes, adjusts his pillow and says, "Hey,

there's my girl. How was school?" Same routine, same answer.

"Good."

He grabs the remote, looks at the clock, and changes the channel.

"You want some nachos?" I say as I pull out the cheese and chips. Communicating from the kitchen to the living room is not a difficult thing to do in our small house.

"Nah. You go ahead."

I stick my plate in the microwave and make no mention of the cut-off notice. What good would it do? Heading to my room, I decide to call Cass, knowing she'll make me feel better.

"I don't know why I ever thought I could pull this thing off. I should've never tried out. It was such a *stupid* idea. There's no way in hell I'll be able to afford cheer this year. No way."

"Chelsea. Chill. You'll make it work somehow. You always do. Look, you know I'll help you as much as I can."

"I don't want your help, Cass. Thank you, but just, no. What I want is for my dad to get motivated for once in his life." I look to make sure my bedroom door is completely closed. "I mean, just for once, could he take care of things? It gets so old."

Cassidy's mom is in the background telling her that dinner's ready. She's distracted for a second while she tells her mom how many tacos she wants. I picture her mom walking to their rich-people kitchen with granite countertops and layering the meat, lettuce, cheese, and tomatoes on shells for Cassidy. I know their kitchen. Candles, fresh flowers, and a dinner table that's set with designer placemats and heavy, polished silverware. She

6

comes back on the line.

"I get it, Chelsea."

I laugh.

"No you don't. You will *never* get it."

We sit on the line with awkward silence for a few minutes. The thing about Cassidy is she truly feels bad for the situation I'm in. She begged me to try out with her, and although my financial situation is not her fault, I know she feels responsible.

"I'm sorry, Chels. I don't know what to say except that I will help you. You know that. I never use all my lunch money, and I'll just start giving you the change every day. We'll make this work. Stop worrying so much."

I exhale slowly into the receiver.

"I know," I roll over on my bed. "Thanks." It's a nice gesture, but 1. Two dollars a day won't dig me out of my hole, and 2. I'm not taking her money.

That night I lounge around in bed and flip through the channels.

After about twenty minutes of dozing, I come to and realize I've been watching an infomercial. A hair bun thingy that's going to solve life's problems for the busy, working mom of three kids. You just pull your hair up then pin the bun right on top and bam! Ready for work in no time!

Pointing the remote toward my box TV, I channel surf for a good while then stop to watch a poker game being played in Las Vegas. The World Series, or something like that. It's a heated battle between the final two players, and the commentators make it even more intense. The camera gives us a glimpse of the prize money—neat stacks of cash that look like they came straight from a bank vault.

A blonde casino model picks up a bundle and the camera zooms in to show the audience the $100 denomination on the corner of the bill.

This image stays in my head for three days straight.

♥

Although the casino is a half hour drive, mostly highway, it seems to take me all of five minutes to get there. I can see the flashing lights from the interstate and my car and heart accelerate simultaneously. When I take the exit, I wonder why they would build such a thing out in the middle of nowhere. There's absolutely nothing else around but a single gas station across the street. A sign displaying a picture of their latest big winner, my guess is a truck driver, flashes the words, "I won $37,000!"

I wheel in as if I know what I'm doing and drive around to take a look.

The place is packed; there's hardly an empty parking space in sight. An elderly couple walks arm-in-arm to their car, and they look as if they're leaving a funeral. Obvious non-winners.

I troll the parking lot and decide to park in back. I sit for a while and take in my surroundings. A security guard in a bright yellow shirt rides around on his bicycle. Why is there security in a parking lot? Do people break into cars out here? Or could he be looking for underage gamblers trying to sneak in?

Breathe in. Hold it, hold it, hold it.

Breathe out. Blow it out.

I collect my thoughts for a few minutes and throw sunglasses on top of my head, figuring they will make me look a little more confident, somehow. That's what grown-ups do, right?

I stretch up to my rear view mirror and apply lip liner, add a touch more eyeliner in the corners of my eyes, and use my index finger to wipe my front teeth. I stare at myself in the mirror. Can I get in? Do I look eighteen? I get this idea that I should have bought a pack of cigarettes to give my age a boost. Because obviously anyone who is old enough to smoke would be old enough to get into a casino, right? I wouldn't necessarily have to smoke them, but if I hold a pack as I walk in the poker room, it may just seal the deal that I'm eighteen.

I dig my keys back out of my purse, start my car, and head to the gas station. If the gas station worker will sell me cigarettes, then I can walk into the casino with no questions asked. I turn the radio up, then off. Then back on again. I slip my compact car into the front space, and hope for the best.

I take another deep breath, walk straight to the counter, and look at the cigarettes behind him. I have no idea what the names of any of them are, so I just point to a white box.

"I'll take a pack of those."

And without blinking he mumbles, "ID."

It wasn't "Ma'am, may please see your ID?" or "Can I take a look at your ID?" It was a cold, hard, from the bottom of his fat belly, "ID."

I open my clutch as if I have one in there. I thumb through my things hoping my school ID isn't exposed . . .

"You know what? I'm *so* sorry. I left it at home. Is there any way you can just take my word on it this time? I'll bring back my ID and show you tomorrow if I need to."

And without a word—without even making eye contact with me, he grabs the cigarettes back off the counter and returns them to their home on the shelf.

"Sir, I can bring it back tomorrow, seriously. I'm old enough to smoke." I'm at his mercy, and no doubt, he likes the power.

Still wordless, besides the "ID," he shows me who won by ringing up the slushy for the kid that stands behind me.

"Gee, thanks." I all but sprint to my car.

I'm stressed, but I don't let it stop me. After all, my dad shares the guy's occupation, and I know my dad would never sell cigarettes to someone underage.

Forget the cigs. Stupid idea anyway.

And in one smooth, uninterrupted motion, before I even have time to think about it, I'm back in the casino parking lot, getting out of my car, and walking through the back entrance along with a half dozen other people.

I have the urge to touch my forehead, my heart, and both shoulders, in a Catholic kind of way, and I'm not even Catholic. My heart's pounding, and when I walk through the second set of glass doors, the smell of cigarette smoke takes my breath away. Literally. My eyes begin to water. I take a quick look and am surprised to see no one checking ID at the door. However, the feeling of everyone looking at me makes me a nervous wreck.

The ringing of the slot machines is continuous, and I wonder how much these people are actually winning. After spotting the sign, I make a beeline for the restroom so I can regroup and get my bearings.

I need deep breaths to calm down, but it is just next to impossible with the funk in the air. And the air just gets funkier when I walk into the bathroom.

A lady two heads shorter than me walks out of her stall and goes straight to the mirrors and sink. I enter my stall, even though I don't need to use it, and lay toilet paper down on the seat. I crouch down and sit there for a little bit, hoping she can't hear my heart that's beating out of my chest. I wait.

Am I really doing this? Am I really going to go out there and try this?

The lady scuffles around. She takes an extra long time to wash her hands, and I picture her fluffing her white beehive hairdo. I sit still on the toilet and listen, then angle my position to look under my stall door. Finally, her silver ballet slippers make an exit. I close my eyes.

You are eighteen.

You are eighteen.

You are eighteen. I tell myself this until I believe it. Then I open my eyes.

I flush. I wash. I reenter the floor.

Lots of action here, in the middle of nowhere, Oklahoma.

I walk around and slip in and out of rows of slot machines for a few minutes. While I familiarize myself with the place, I see a line of senior citizens waiting for a dinner buffet to open, a couple high-fiving to a modest win, and pictures of familiar faces like Vanna White inviting me to come play their slot machines. A center bar serves a few customers as they take swigs of draft beer and play an electronic something or another.

Tucked neatly in a corner, I find the poker room. So I sit at a slot machine that's near, dig around in my purse, and pretend to play. Slot machines are sheer luck, a risk I can't take. Fortunately, I have a skill. Like an FBI agent, I watch every move in the room.

The cocktail waitresses with their spilling cleavages don't intimidate me. The dealers with their tacky white oxfords and bowties don't scare me, nor do the players, mostly males, average age sixty-five. But there's this stud in a suit wearing an earpiece who's obviously not listening to music. Just like the casino movies, he's watching for scammers and bad guys; I just know it. Standing with his back against the wall, arms crossed, he acts like he owns the place. He talks into a little mouthpiece, and I'm dying to know who he's talking to and what it is they're saying. Probably talking to the mob boss upstairs, and probably saying, "We gotta underage on the Money Bags slot machine. Move in. Let's get 'er." I turn away, and then look out of the corner of my eye.

A giant computerized waiting list hangs above the check-in desk, and all existing poker games are listed. IMMEDIATE SEATING flashes under the 3-6 limit game, and I wonder what that means. The man sporting a 'stache at the front desk picks up the microphone, interrupting "Little Red Corvette" playing in the background.

"Chuck, your 5-10 seat is now available. Chuck." He places the microphone down on the desk.

A cute little whippersnapper, I'd guess to be in his eighties, appears in no time. He takes off his glasses, cleans them with his shirt, and scoots to his place at a table. There's a low buzz of conversation in the room, and the clicking of poker chips echoes from players fidgeting by stacking and restacking.

I busy myself, once again, by digging randomly in my purse.

You are eighteen. You are eighteen.

I discretely look around—all around—turning my head slowly to locate cameras disguised in starburst décor. I've seen it on TV before. Casinos have hidden cameras everywhere, in ceiling tiles, plants, decorations; they're all over the place. "Eye in the sky" is what they call it. I sit for a few more minutes inhaling and exhaling slowly. Finally, I silence my cell, close my purse, and walk straight up to the 'stache guy. Over his shoulder I see a fuzzy blend of green felt tables, a cashier window in the back, and a reach-in refrigerator stocked with bottled water.

I speak first. "3-6 limit, please." My hands stay in my pockets to make sure no one can see them shake. No WAY will they find out I am a virgin poker-room girl.

"Seat right over there, ma'am." He points to a table in the corner.

His calling me "ma'am" reassures me. So far, so good.

And faster than you can say royal flush, my ass is in a chair. I'm seeing visions in my head of Poker Boss in the back walking over, asking for ID, then calling for back up in his mic. Please don't let that happen. Please.

I set my purse by my feet and scoot my chair closer to the table. I'm sandwiched nicely between an old lady with offensively bright red hair and an Asian guy. I join the table in the middle of a hand, and I sit on my hands in attempt to make them stop shaking.

"All in." An old fart dripping with gold and exposed gray chest fuzz says from the end of the table.

"Charlie. Charlie. Charlie. Why do ya have to do that to me?" A not-as-flashy old guy responds. I stare at the community cards in the middle and wonder who's got what. It's immediately obvious that the people on this table are on a first name basis, and I'm in need of a sticky nametag.

Cozy Pops with a trucker hat and Flashy Grandpa engage in a stare down, and I get the feeling this isn't the first time. The dealer reaches over to count the "All In" chips . . . a total of forty-two dollars.

"Forty-two to call," he says.

Charlie clicks his teeth and stares over at the cocktail waitress wearing next to nothing. A long, hard stare, which tells me he's trying to remove himself from the hand he's right in the middle of. Hmm . . . Possible bluff?

Cozy Pops reads the bluff and pushes his forty-two over the line.

"I call."

Charlie responds under his breath, "Son-of-a . . ." And throws his cards face down to the dealer. Doesn't even show them to compete, and I'm already fond of Cozy Pops for calling his bluff.

Cozy Pops exposes his cards, jack/ten, and they match up nicely to the jack and ten in the community cards. Two pair for Pops.

Wow.

The dealer pushes a mound of colorful chips over to Cozy Pops, and Pops throws back one red one. Maybe a tip?

Wow.

The dealer, out of breath and rockin' the scale at a minimum of three hundred, shuffles the cards, not in a traditional bridge-falling-down style, but rather he turns them all face down and scoots them around with his fingers as if he's a little kid with finger paints. That's interesting. You'd think they would hire dealers who know how to shuffle.

Too scared to make eye contact with my opponents, I stare down the dealer during his shuffle. His employee identification card claims he's Mike Tanner, and the picture to prove it was taken about ten years ago. In the previous decade Mike was thinner and his hair was all pepper, no salt.

He scares me to death when he comes to a stop in the middle of his shuffle/finger painting and looks right at me. "Welcome to the game, Blondie. Need some chips?" The only bills I possess are five twenties that came straight from my credit union Savables account. Remaining balance: twenty-seven dollars.

I pull out all five bills—crisp and sticky—and place them on the table.

"Yeah, I'll take some chips."

"CASHING A HUNDRED," Dealer Mike yells across the room, which makes me jump.

Nice.

If jumping in your chair doesn't scream casino virgin, I don't know what does.

He takes my cash, wads and wrinkles it, then places it under a row of chips. It's like he's the banker in a game of Monopoly with that tray of vertical chips in neat rows.

No time for chat, he moves right on to the next hand. Cards start flying across the green felt and all of a sudden each player has two cards facedown.

Everyone starts to peek at their cards and I do the same.

Ace of spades.

Three of hearts.

Then I return my hands back under my legs.

This is a decent start, but I don't know how the hell to participate. What does 3-6 limit mean, exactly? I wait patiently and let it unfold. Although we play with the same fifty-two-card deck, the rules of engagement seem to be a bit more sophisticated than a friendly game at home.

♠

A heap of pennies sat in the middle of our glass table. Dad took a drink of his Coke and sat it back down on the folded paper towel that served as a coaster. He stared into my eyes. "Listen here, Pigtails. Don't think you can bully me into giving up this four of a kind I'm holding." He squinted and pretended to get serious.

Dad knew I didn't bluff. If I placed a bet, I had something. Something good. My eyes followed the numbers for a second time to make sure I had what I thought I had. Seven. Eight. Nine. Ten. Jack. Sure enough, they were all there. Dad himself had taught me to never move my hold cards around to make sure of my hand.

"Daddy," I giggled. "You don't have a four of a kind. It's not nice to lie."

Dad took the cards he held and moved them around. "Let's see. Ace. Ace. Ace . . ." He moved one last card closer to his eyes. "Yep, it's an Ace."

I laughed harder.

"Daddy, you don't have Aces!"

"Well, how much are you willing to bet?" Dad nodded to my pennies.

I counted them out into stacks of five then pushed four stacks to the middle. "Twenty cents."

Dad gasped.

"*Twenty cents!*" He rested his forehead into his palm and went into his exaggerated deep-thinking mode. "*Twenty cents, you say?*"

I swung my legs back and forth in my chair and blew my bangs off my forehead.

"*Yep. Twenty cents.*"

"*Are you surrrre you wanna do that?*" Scare tactics were his go-to move. "*I mean twenty cents would take over half your stack if you lost.*"

"*Daddy. The bet is twenty cents. Call or fold.*"

He stacked his pennies in groups of tens. Then waited a couple minutes contemplating whether he should push them to the middle or not. "*Well, I don't see how there's any way you could beat these four aces I'm holding.*" He looked up really quick to see my reaction.

I leaned into the table and gave him a long, hard stare.

"*Well I think you're bluffing,*" Dad laughed and pushed his pennies to the middle. "*I'll call your bluff.*"

I jumped up on my knees and revealed each card one at a time.

"*Read 'em and weep! I've got a seven. Eight. Niiiiine. Ten. And jack.*" I slapped my hand on the table.

Dad peered down at the cards.

"*Well what do you call that?*"

"*A straight, Daddy! I have a straight!*"

He inspected the cards using his pointer finger to scoot each one as he named them.

"*Well, well. A straight indeed-y.*" Dad looked down at his cards then scratched his head. "*Wait a minute! Where'd my aces go?*"

He tossed his cards down for me to see.

"*Daddy I knew you were bluffing!*"

I stood in my chair, stretched across the table and scooped up the pennies, knocking the neat stacks over toward my end of the table.

Dad watched patiently as my little fingers built towers of pennies. I rested my chin on the table and marveled at the tall stacks. He stood, in true poker fashion, and clapped his hands together just once to pull me from my jubilation.

"Ante up, Pigtails."

Chapter 3

Before I know it, the bet has moved around to me.

"Three to call, little lady."

Little. That implies I look young, which is not a good thing.

A man appears with a small rack of 100 one dollar chips and sets them in front of me. And I can't bring myself to answer the dealer.

He repeats, "Three to call."

Nerves get the best of me and I respond.

"Um. I'm out."

Red Head Lady to my left is extremely put out with me. I don't know if it's because I've slowed down the game or because I've invaded her one to seven women/men ratio.

She throws in her chips, and she's in the game looking for some action. As the bet moves around the table she points to my cards and says, "You need to throw those back in to the dealer." Not in a sweet, "I'm-here-to-help-you" way, rather a "you-are-already-on-my-nerves" way.

So I toss the cards back in then retuck my hands.

Suited-up Mafia Guy starts moving our direction, and I don't know whether to make a mad dash for the door or apply more lipstick. CRAP.

The hand continues, and I'm completely oblivious to what's going on because The Suit is getting closer and closer.

You are eighteen. You are eighteen. You are eighteen.

He finally reaches our table, and walks straight behind me.

Seriously?!

There's no way he knows I'm underage. No way.

"Ma'am, can I get your rack?"

EXCUSE ME??!! I give him a blank stare, and I know way down deep that I'm busted. Visions of jail bars make a quick appearance in my brain.

He points down to my poker chips and says, "I can get that out of your way."

Ohhhhh, poker chip rack. I get it now.

"Sure, thanks." I start unloading my chips onto the felt table making a mess, knocking over stacks, the whole nine yards. After what feels like days later, I hand him the empty plastic rack and say, "Thanks." I smile.

He smiles, then turns to walk away.

Cute guy . . . in a *Sopranos* kind of way.

By the time I focus back on the game, I already have two cards facedown and we're onto the next hand.

Queen of hearts. Queen of spades.

Figuring out the casino's betting system suddenly becomes urgent. I know how to play poker. A pair of queens in the hole is really good. The bet comes around to me, and Asian Guy on my right throws in a red five dollar chip and a white, one dollar chip. I count out six ones and throw them to the pot before the dealer can even look up, proving to the table that I'm a very fast learner.

Chips and cards fly around, then the dealer tidies up the pot and pounds the table twice with his fist.

He turns three community cards up, and I swear I'm seeing things. Two. Queen. Four.

My shaky hands are suddenly convulsing, and I wonder how I'm even going to handle picking up my chips.

No one bets for a while . . . until Asian Guy. He makes a statement when he throws in the limit—a red and a white, six bucks, and they scatter across the table. Either he's very, very confident or he's really, really bluffing.

I can't catch my breath. It's my turn. Wishing I had some red chips to make this easier, I start to count out twelve white ones. I'm embarrassed—no, humiliated, because my hands are jolting at a ridiculous level at this point. I finally complete my task and scoot them across the line.

"I call and raise six dollars." My words are weak and shaky. I need to win this pot, I really, really need it, but just continued breathing will suffice at the moment.

Everyone at the table folds, but Asian Guy gives it one last go. He does the same: call and raise. Luckily, this time I don't have to speak. I toss in my twelve bucks.

The dealer turns over the next community card. Two. My eyes widen.

That gives me a full house. Full house equals . . . Ohmygosh! I'M GOING TO WIN THIS THING.

I become entranced, staring at the pot. I've been on this table less than five minutes, and I'm already about to take one down.

The bet is on my opponent. He doesn't hesitate.

"I check."

What? I thought he had something!

He's testing me. That's the only thing I can figure.

I can't give him the stare down because he's seated next to me. The thought crosses my mind that he's holding a pair of twos in his hands, four of a kind, which would beat me.

I let out a nervous giggle trying to buy time. How in the hell am I supposed to play this?!

I look at the pot and think of the cheer shoes I am in such desperate need of. Here goes nothing . . .

"Six dollars." I push my white chips to the middle in disbelief that this has all happened so fast. I may not be eating for a month, but I'm all in.

My job is done. There's nothing left to say. It's all up to my opponent.

He rattles something under his breath, looks at his hand, and starts to tap his cards up and down. This is a huge relief. If he had four twos there's *no* way he'd be thinking this over.

He continues the rattle and tap, and Red Head Lady next to me strikes up a conversation with Dealer Mike about the crab legs on the buffet.

"They're no good," she says.

Mike agrees about the crab legs then forces the game to continue.

"Six to call, Phong."

He taps his cards one last time then begins to count

out his chips.

He pauses one last time to take one last look at his cards, then places his neat stacks of chips over the line.

Holy Joker. He's going for it.

"Let's see 'em." Mike waves toward me first.

I flip over my cards to reveal my gem of a hand.

Mike raises his eyebrows and he's more shocked than I am.

"Full house, queens full of twos."

Phong flips his over to reveal a flush.

The dealer starts pushing the chips my way, and I force my body to stiffen like a statue for the next several minutes. We're already into the next hand when I finally come to and start to stack my chips. Including the antes and previous rounds of betting, it's a nice little heap of chips. I can't even focus on the current hand because I'm replaying the last hand in my head over and over at a very fast rate. The scary thing? I had no idea that Phong had that good of a hand. A flush? *No* idea. I should've paid more attention that that was even a possibility. A flush wins like 110 percent of the time.

I'm still a nervous wreck, and I'm ready to get the heck out of this place.

The bets on me, and I barely give my cards a glance and throw them in.

I'm done.

I'm like, *more* than done.

My attention is suddenly split between my win and Mafia Guy, who just walked past the table again. He's . . . *cuuute*. Older than me, definitely, but not by much. He looks about twenty-one. Maybe twenty-two, but he can't be older than that. I stare when he's not looking so he doesn't catch me. He makes his way to the corner of the room to help a player who looks to be at least ninety. He lets the old man grab the crook of his arm, and together they walk very, very, very slowly across the room and out the door. So sweet and patient.

After a few more hands, and a couple of wins, I think of Dad at home probably beginning to wonder where I'm at.

Looking around for a cashier, I try to figure out how to carry these chips since Cute Mafia Guy took my chip tray. Do I just start loading them in my purse? Or can you do that? I spot the cashier window, and decide it will look ridiculous if I make three trips back and forth to get my chips up there. Once again, I'm letting everyone know about my newbie status.

Hmm.

Surely I won't be the first one to ever ask . . . I look at the dealer.

"Mike, can I get one of those tray things back?"

Flashy Grandpa takes it upon himself to respond, "Oh. You're not leaving us are ya? You just got started!" Everyone waits for my response. A lie formulates in my brain shockingly fast.

"I've got to get to work."

"Well, you'll have to come back when you can stay longer." He manages to say all this while playing poker and throwing in chips at the same time.

"I will. Thanks." Oh I will, all right.

Mike motions for someone to bring me a tray, and Cute Mafia Guy starts to make his way over.

He smiles at me as he approaches. *Very* cute. Dimples, shaved head, big brown eyes.

I'm embarrassed when one tray isn't enough, and he goes back to the cashier's cage to get another. He brings me the second one in a rush because there's some kind of commotion/dispute going on at another table. Perfect for me, because that leaves us no time to talk. I fill the trays, tuck my clutch under my arm, and begin to make my way out. I can't help but smile the whole way to the cashier.

The cashier, with hair sprayed up to Jesus and nine long red fingernails (one broken), counts my chips and opens her cash drawer. She counts my money, fans it on the counter, then shows her empty hands to what I'm assuming is an "eye in the sky."

Oh yeah, baby! It's all mine. Hello, electricity. HEL-LO new cheer shoes. No time for placing it neatly in my wallet, I fold it once and stuff it in my purse. Turning to make my exit, I literally run straight into Cute Mafia Guy.

He gently grabs my arm and says, "Got a minute?"

Chapter 4

Oh, SHIT. He knows. I know he knows.

My first thought is that I hope they will let me keep my winnings to use for bail money. My dad *cannot* afford to bail me out of jail.

We're interrupted with some talk in his earpiece and he loosens his hold on my arm. I wonder if he's always this calm making apprehensions.

Can I outrun him?

No way. This place is probably crawling with security.

I wait quietly but impatiently until finally he says, "Can I get your name?"

This is it. I'm busted.

I can't even look at him.

"Ch—Chandra Simmons." I can hardly get it out.

"Is this your first time here?" He asks.

I come back quickly, "Uh, yeah. I usually play in the casinos back home."

"Oh. Where's home?"

And I can't come up with an answer. How am I

supposed to know which towns have casinos?

"Out of state," is the only thing I can come up with. I continue, "I just moved here not too long ago."

Will I be handcuffed?

He points the other way, "Well, Chandra, let me get you set up with a Players' Club Card. That way you can earn points for free meals when you play. That lady right over there will help you." He points to a lady that could pass for the cashier's twin.

My luck didn't stop at the poker table. Thankyou. Thankyou. Thank. You.

I smile.

"Hey, thanks. I'll do that next time; I'm kind of in a hurry."

He adjusts his blazer lapel and says, "Oh, alrighty. We'll see ya next time then, Chandra."

It's odd that a guy that could play a part in *The Sopranos* would use the word "alrighty," but maybe his suit and earpiece aren't indicative of who he really is. Interesting.

I walk briskly to my car. When I step outside, the oxygen feels extra crisp and clean. A blue truck begins to follow me down the row of parked cars, and this makes me pick up my pace. I make eye contact with the driver. He's a clean-cut guy wearing a baseball hat.

Wait, but serial killers can look clean-cut.

Or what if he's an undercover cop coming to arrest me?

I move even faster. When I get to my car I can hardly get my keys out of my purse. Between the poker win and this, my hands aren't functioning as they should, and I drop my keys on the ground. I hurry and pick them up, then force my hand to get the *freaking* key in the keyhole. Finally, I jump in my car and lock the doors. My eyes dart back to the blue truck. He's got his blinker on, waiting for my space. He pulls his hand up off the steering wheel and waves. I blow out a long breath then back my car out.

After I leave, I'm still in disbelief that this whole thing happened so I pull over at the gas station parking lot under a light to count my cash and make sure it's for real.

394 freakin' dollars. $294 more than I had before. For real.

That just happened.

Wow!

Bye-bye cutoff notice. Plus, I'll buy new jeans. I need some jewelry. It's name-brand cereal this week. Coke instead of water—I'll splurge on the good stuff. Hair products. I'll buy hair products! Like the ones that Cassidy and all the other girls use. My hair will be shiny and gorgeous like theirs. Even *smell* expensive. I KNOW! I'll go to the salon and get my hair done by a hairdresser! An actual hairdresser!

♣

"Honey, come here. Let's try to brush out these knots. You can't go to school with a bunch of knots now, can you?" Dad waved me over with his comb.

I shook my head no, buckled my sandal, and headed toward the sink and mirror. I saw my reflection. My sun-bleached hair looked as if it had gotten caught up in the bottom of a vacuum cleaner.

Dad ran the water and wet the comb, then went to work.

"Ouch! DAD! OUCH! You're hurting me!"

Dad rubbed my scalp with his fingers. "I'm sorry, honey, but these things have to be brushed out."

He rewet the comb.

It hurt badly. "OUCH!" Tears flooded my eyes.

"Honey, I know it hurts. Just give me a second here."

He yanked some more.

I cried some more.

After minutes of agonizing yanking, my hair lay against my head, wet strands free of tangles.

I slid my palm down my hair. My cry came to an end, and I caught my breath in between words. "Can . . . I . . . have . . . a ponytail?"

"A what?" Dad asked sympathetically.

"A ponytail. Like Mama used to do." I watched his face in the mirror. He looked around the vanity area knowing there wasn't a rubber band in sight.

"Stay right here."

I watched myself sniffle and take quick breaths, and continued flattening my wet hair with my palm.

"A ponytail it is, my little first grader," he happily chanted from the other room. I heard him walk out the front door then walk back in.

He returned with the newspaper and pulled off the rubber band. I smiled with wet, red eyes, and faced the mirror once more.

"Be real still." Dad was determined. He wet the comb one last time, and slicked me down for a low pony.

"Let's see here." Awkwardly, he wrapped the newspaper rubber band around my hair until the ponytail was complete.

"Voilà!" He pointed the comb at my head as if he just made a rabbit appear then broke out in song. "Hereeee sheeee issssss: Misssss Americaaa . . ."

The movies. I'll go to the movies and actually pay for a ticket. I'll get popcorn. Popcorn, candy, and a Coke. Or a good bra. From the mall! I can buy a good bra! One where the wire doesn't come out and poke me all day long. Or expensive sunglasses. Or a flat iron! A mani/pedi, that's what I'll do with this money! Mani/pedi!

I spend the money 3 million ways in my head.

Or maybe . . . *just* maybe . . . I could get my picture taken. By, like, a professional or something. Like the other girls do. Gorgeous background, an edited smile in an expensive frame. Finally! It will be rich in color, for sure. Expensive looking. I like that one of Cassidy at the botanical gardens with water in the background. I could do that. I could totally do that! *Cheeeeeeeese.*

I smile all the way home.

Chapter 5

By the next cheer practice, I walk in a new woman. I can literally feel the stares at my feet and sense the other girls thinking, "Well it's about time." Everyone else has had their white leather cheer shoes for some time now, while I've practiced in my white/turning yellow canvas ones.

And just like little kids that run faster with new shoes, I cheer better. The shoes are way lighter than my heavy, clunky things, and my kicks just seem to go a little higher. We practice for two hours, and it marks the first time I actually feel like part of the team. Don't really know if it has anything to do with the shoes, but things are just clicking. I remember the choreography. I hit stunts. My jumps are rockin'. I'm soaring high, and the thought of being crowned Homecoming Queen while wearing a fancy dress makes a quick appearance in my head.

Now that I've got my shoes, I'm thinking I *really* need the $120 pair of jeans I saw the other day. And that would take me, what . . . an hour on the poker table?

"Let's run the dance one more time and then we're outta here." Rylee, the cheer captain, leads us into the dance again. The music begins to thump, and I go through the motions because I am too excited about my soon-to-be new jeans to think about anything else. Rhinestones or no rhinestones? Decisions, decisions . . .

Should I go back tonight? The fact that I was just at the casino two nights ago makes me a bit nervous. But then again, the casino peeps should remember me and not bother to ask for ID . . . right?

After the dance, Rylee jumps in front, faces us, and readjusts her headband.

"Practice again tomorrow. If you haven't paid choreography fees to Miss Mound yet, do it by the end of next week. Good practice today! Can't wait for football season!" She claps her hands, and the group of ponytails disperses to grab their bags and water bottles.

Shit. Choreography fees.

I've got my work cut out for me. For sure.

Choreography fees plus rhinestone jeans equals . . . poker. TONIGHT.

I check my phone, grab my bag, and head for the parking lot. The days are still long, and the sun is still shining. I trot across the parking lot to my lonely car, and wonder if I could win enough to buy me a new one. Well, of course I could!

I throw my things on top of a pile of junk that sits upon more junk. Random stuff that, at a glimpse, would make me appear to be a packrat. *America's Junkiest Cars.* Now there's a reality show waiting to happen. Sunglasses, umbrella, empty chip bag, and I know my geography binder is under there somewhere.

Anticipating the check-in call to Dad, I start to consider my lie options.

I'm going to the library. Nah.

I'll be at Cassidy's. No. He drives by her house on the way to his night shift.

I'm washing my car. Nah.

I'm going to Walmart for some personal items. Now there's something he won't question.

As I pull out of the school parking lot, I hold one hand on the steering wheel and dig around in my purse for my phone with the other. When I find the little, cheap thing, I decide that with my future abundant poker winnings, a smart phone is definitely on the "to buy" list.

"Hey, Dad. What's up?"

"Just put a gourmet dinner in the oven. I'm trying a new recipe. Are you comin' home?"

"Dad, frozen pepperoni pizza is not a recipe."

He laughs.

"It is when you add extra Parmesan cheese."

Here it goes.

"I won't be home until later. I need to run by Wal-Mart for some personal things, and it may take a while." No matter how close I am to my dad, the mention of personal things is ten kinds of awkward.

"Oh okay, honey. Do you still have that twenty I gave you last week?"

That twenty was gone in two days.

"Yeah, Dad. I'll use that. It'll be plenty."

"Alright, honey. If you don't get home before I leave, be careful and call me before you go to bed."

"I will. Love you, Dad."

"Love you too, honey."

That was easy.

I'm two miles into the drive before I decide my cheer practice clothes won't cut it in a casino. Although there's no picture of a mascot, anyone could look at my clothes and pin me a cheerleader. But I can't go home to change.

I have $102. I need every cent of that for the poker table, which rules out stopping to buy a new shirt.

Unless I go to Goodwill, a place Dad and I frequent from time to time.

I head for the store and brainstorm how I'm going to wash a shirt without going home. This could be complicated. When I walk in, it's the same, familiar, old lady perfume stench. It's crowded, and there's a screaming kid on the loose with no apparent supervision. Flipping through the clothes, I look for the one with the least amount of snot, lint, or crust.

A long sleeved button-up should suffice. That way I can keep my t-shirt on and wear it as a jacket, and the dirtiness will only touch my skin from the elbows down. A pretty lavender plaid will do for $2.49. Although the shirt will be on my body in twenty short minutes, I don't allow it to touch any part of my car, like it has cooties or something. I tuck the bag into the floorboard, away from my other stuff.

As I drive to the casino, I am over-the-top excited. I can't get there fast enough.

Is this the same high you get from smoking pot?

I park in the back because I know what I'm doing. I reach down for the shirt. Usually when I wash a thrift store shirt I switch the washing machine setting to hot and use an extra scoop of detergent. *Never* have I put on a shirt straight from the bag.

I pull it out.

Ew . . . I remove the price tag using my teeth. EW.

Then I shake it out and pull it on.

Ew.

Ew. Ew. Ew. EW.

I feel as if bugs are crawling into my hair. To escape it, I repeatedly squirt mango body spray all over myself and hurry up and get out of the car.

When I walk up and see Cute Mafia Guy is working the poker room, I disappear to the bathroom before he sees me. I double check my makeup, powder my face, and then take a long look at myself in the full-length mirror. I remove my ponytail holder and tease my hair to bring it in front of my shoulders. The Goodwill shirt looks wrinkly, like I pulled it straight from the hamper. If only. To make the best of it, I tie it up at the waist.

There's no waiting list for my table, so I'm immediately seated. I can't seem to catch my breath. I was expecting a little wait time.

Cards are flying, and I don't recognize any of the players from the other night. I need Cozy Pops back. I pull the $100 bill from my purse, and the dealer—a man who apparently forgot his morning shave—hollers, "Changing $100." He stuffs my bill into a slit in the table so I'll forget it ever existed.

When I reach across the table to scoot my chips closer, I get a whiff of my shirt. *Ohmygosh*. Beyond stinky. Hopefully the cigarette smoke will overpower me.

It's arctic freezing in the poker room, and the combination of my nerves and frozenness makes me stiffen my body to refrain from jolting. I quickly look away after Cute Mafia Guy and I make eye contact. Now he knows I'm here. He knows I know he's here. I run my hand through my hair then look over at him again. He's talking to a player wearing a baseball cap, but he's still looking at me. This makes me shake even more.

My chip pile looks tiny because it's all red five dollar chips. My competitors, however, have mounds of color in front of them. I take a deep breath and start to examine their faces. No smiles. Strictly business. With some empty seats at the table, it's me and three males.

The dealer looks at me then begins his routine of mix, stack, and deal. The players exchange looks, and a couple of them even look at my stack of chips. I've already been assessed and determined fresh meat, and this increases my heart rate. A gent that could pass for a preacher opens the betting with six dollars, a bit arrogant for the first round.

My hand sucks so I toss in the cards and wait patiently for the next hand. Meanwhile, my eyes dart around, searching for Cute Mafia Guy. He's talking to the regulars, and I can tell he's gradually making his way over to my table. Two tables over, the extra tan, extra cleavage-y cocktail waitress is reaching over to deliver a Budweiser, and I hope he's not seeing what I am. They're probably sleeping together. It's probably his longtime girlfriend, and she's waitressing to work her way through med school, and they probably have plans to get married, have four gorgeous kids, and live in a two-story house with a pool so she can lounge around in her string bikini while he does cannonballs to splash her.

Really, he's too old for me anyway.

I look for gum in my purse while the last hand ends and the next one begins.

"Hey, I see you're back." A hand touches my back.

I jump as if a gun has been fired and there he is, and God, is he cute.

"Oh, yeah, just getting a few hands in before I go to the store." Did that sound grown-up?!

He smiles. Dimples, dark eyes, buzz cut, perfect suit. I'm trying to figure out whose turn it is to talk. I'm too entranced for my brain to function normally. I feel the cards hit my hands and take a peek. King/jack. *Come to mama.*

He touches my back again.

"Well I'll let you get down to business. Good luck."

I throw my cards to the dealer, and turn around to catch him before he walks off.

"Well," I glance down at his nametag. Nate Bradley. "Looks like I'm going to need some luck tonight."

"Don't we all," the old man sitting next to me butts in. Nate chuckles and walks away to do casino-y stuff. I hate myself for throwing away a good hand in exchange for one chuckle. I can't let it go . . . King, jack, king, jack, king, jack. I want a do-over.

The hand unfolds as the pot grows and another king comes up.

Chapter 6

Three hours later I'm down to eight bucks, and I make myself get up and leave. If my gas tank wasn't nearly empty I'd give it one last shot, but I can't risk losing any more with a thirty-minute drive home.

My breathing is shallow, I'm numb, and I hate myself for losing ninety-two dollars. I keep my eyes on Nate and strategically slip out when he has his back turned. He has probably figured out by now that I wasn't exactly on my way to the "grocery store." I rush to get out and trip over a lady's purse as I find my way out of the poker room.

Everyone in this whole place looks like they're attending a funeral. The constant ring of the slot machines is such a hoax. No one in this whole damn place is winning. I pay close attention to the pitiful cases as I walk toward the doors.

A grandma losing her retirement.

A mechanic losing his kid's lunch money.

A college kid losing his tuition.

This is sick. I'm never coming back. Never. Ever. Never

again.

When I walk out into the world of smoke-free oxygen, I'm glad the charade is over.

It's dark, so I jog to my car in hopes that I don't get mugged. When my doors are locked, I hug my steering wheel for a second, glad to be back in my real life.

I'll just quit the squad. Things could be worse. There are kids without shoes and shelter and I'm stressed about a freakin' cheer choreography fee.

I pull away from the flashing light and head across the street to pump gas. I grab my purse and go into the store that smells of Cheetos and candy. True to my luck of the night, the same big belly worker is behind the counter. There's no cup of courtesy pennies on the counter, so I just hand him my eight bucks. He pops open his register and is put-out to count forty-nine cents because he has to break open a roll of pennies. I, however, enjoy it.

On my way home I replay the hand I could have won.

I had it won. Miguel, as they called him, intimidated me with his high bets every round. I knew I had him beat. Why didn't I stay in? He didn't have crap. Or did he? I should have stayed in to force him to show his hand. I need another re-do. Why didn't I bet the maximum early in the hand? It would've built a bigger pot.

Thirty minutes of woulda-coulda-shouldas and I make my way home and pull into the driveway.

I lost ninety-two dollars.

Good GRIEF, just let it go.

NINETY-TWO FREAKIN' DOLLARS.

I will never. Never. Ever. Go back again.

Chapter 7

After six hours in bed but hardly any sleep, I get up and make my way to the shower. The sun is beaming through the small window that's neatly covered with thin, yellow curtains, curtains that we've had since I can remember, curtains that I'm sure Mom probably picked out herself. The towels and dirty clothes are still piled on the floor from yesterday—yet another reminder that I am a loser. Had I stayed home last night, I'd have a cabinet of neatly folded towels and ninety-two dollars still in my purse.

I start the water, undress, and grab a washcloth. As I get in, my hair receives the steam, and WHOA the cigarette smell is back. The smoke oozes from my skin cells, and it's nauseating. I breathe through my mouth to keep from smelling last night's debacle.

I'm tired.

I want nothing more than to wash this smoke off my body and go back to bed. Maybe I could dream of Mom and picnics, and maybe she could give me some advice as to how to get myself out of this predicament.

What would she say?

Quit the cheer squad?

Don't give up?

Find an honest job?

Lighten your load?

I need direction.

I turn the water off and step out of the steam. I sit down on the tub, and all of the sudden I'm six again. In the tub.

"Dad?"

"Yeah?"

"Will we ever get a new Mama?"

He stops washing my hair, frozen for just a few seconds. "What do you mean?"

"Will we ever get a new Mama? Or do we just have to wait and see if ours comes back?"

He takes the showerhead from the handle, and tests the water temperature on his hands. "Lean back."

He rinses the shampoo then applies the conditioner.

"Lean back, kiddo. You're going to get it in your eyes."

I lean back, and he rinses.

He stands and gets a towel from the cabinet, and tosses it onto the floor. "Time to get out." For the first time ever, he leaves me to get out by myself.

Cassidy finds me at my locker before school. The

hallways are sparse—a couple minutes before the tardy bell, and I've already declared myself late since I started cleaning out my locker.

"Where were you last night? I tried to call you. When I came by your house your car wasn't there." I continue pulling out loose papers and tossing them on the floor by my feet.

"When?"

"What do you mean, when? Like all night long." She's irritated.

I start taking my textbooks out one at a time and stacking them neatly on the floor. Lies begin to formulate in my head, and I hesitate a little too long.

"Chelsea! Where were you? I thought you'd been kidnapped or something! I didn't know whether to call your dad at work or what!"

I stop what I'm doing to look at her, and then go back to my cleaning. "I just had a lot of errands and stuff. I went to the store. We were out of everything; it just took me a long time, that's all."

"Why weren't you answering your phone?"

"My battery died . . . shit, back off. I didn't realize you were my keeper." I drop a textbook to the stack—*whack*. I'm not in the mood.

She doesn't respond but stands there looking at me. The bell rings, and she leaves.

I rub my hand across the bottom of my locker to remove the fuzz balls and dust then stack my books back into my locker, this time vertically. I pull my health book from the stack, knowing this new locker organization system will work *so* much better than before.

A locker cleanse.

Just what I needed.

After school I go to practice.

Some are already stretching when I walk into the gym, their hair pulled up in messy buns on top of their heads. The gym is humid and stinks like socks. I go to the locker room and change into my practice clothes, and as I'm tying my cheer shoes, another cheerleader, Reagan, walks in.

I just need a moment.

A moment to decide if I'm going to do this. So I sit down on the locker room bench that's so waxy it looks wet, criss-cross my legs, and slowly start rolling my head around to stretch my neck. I watch Reagan out of the corner of my eye. She has a huge, black, Coach gym bag. It has to be a $400 bag, at least. She sets it on another bench and checks her smartphone.

"Hey, Chelsea."

"Hey," I reply.

She's obviously been tanning. When she slips into her red practice shorts, there's a striking contrast between her brown legs and her white cheer shoes. She tucks her Kate Spade clutch purse into her gym bag, then zips the bag and stacks it long ways into her locker. She uses one hand to push her bag in, and the other hand to close the door, then locks the digital combination lock.

I keep rolling my head and extend my left leg across the bench to stretch my hamstring. Reagan pulls her hair on top of her head without even looking in the mirror. I know just by looking at her that her check for fees has already been written.

"You comin'?" she asks me on her way out the door.

"Yeah, I'll be out there in a sec." But she's already gone.

What am I doing here . . .?

I don't belong.

The door swings open and Cassidy busts in, clearly in a rush. I jump up and start heading for the door. She apologizes for getting on to me this morning and jokes that I'm "grounded." I laugh it off and exit out onto the gym floor. I go through the motions of going through the motions. It's old choreography we're polishing, so my body's on autopilot.

"Sharper! Shaper!" Miss Mound yells 352 times and slips in the occasional "Toes!" or "Formations!"

The practice, to an outsider, would be an ironic joke. The coach couldn't extend her leg— much less make it "sharper" even if she was held at gunpoint and her life depended on it. She is dressed to the hilt, as always. I'm sympathetic to the extra pointy, black, shiny heels she has on, thinking they're going to surrender to the weight above them—and break off and die—any second. Miss Mound . . . She's nice enough, but she is constantly prying into the rich, popular cheerleaders' business. She checks them out head to toe and asks things like, "What ski resort are you staying at?" and "Did your mom get a new Escalade?" and "Where are you shopping for your prom dress?" Every practice she's barking out orders and popping peanut M&Ms at the same time. Except for one day she completely changed it up and was eating Skittles. I caught her reading the nutrition label on the back of the bag. Zero fat in those chewy little candies.

Needless to say, she's never gotten into my business.

She likes me.

As the music plays from her old-school CD player, thunder starts to rip outside, and the already humid air in the gym becomes even heavier. Every move I make takes everything I have because I am so tired from last night. Now would be a good time to go ahead and quit so I could go home and take a nap. But when the coach says we have just one more run through, I decide to hang in there.

We know practice is over when we hear the usual, "Good job, girls." She says it because she has to.

"If you," she pauses due to loud thunder, "haven't paid your choreography fees yet, I need a check today." She looks my direction.

My decision has been made for me.

This has to be it.

In the locker room, I'm slow to pack up my stuff while everyone else is in and out in a flash. I stall by using the bathroom, wash my hands for an extra-long time, and change back into my school clothes. When I walk back out onto the gym floor, she's visiting with the boys' golf coach so I linger and wait my turn.

After a few minutes, Miss Mound says goodbye to the other coach then walks to start turning off the lights.

"What's up, Chelsea?" She asks, continuing her balancing act on those heels.

I take a deep breath.

I double check to make sure we're alone.

"Miss Mound, I don't have the money yet for my fees so I guess I need to quit the squad."

"When will you have it?" She asks.

Wait.

I thought I just quit.

"I just need another week. My dad's waiting on a big bonus at work, and I think he gets it this weekend." I start chewing my thumbnail.

"It's too late to quit . . . It would screw up our formations. I'll talk to the director and see if there's any way we can send your money in a little late. And anyway, you're too good to quit, Chelsea." She knows me, and I think she knows that things don't come easy for me. She likes me because in the materialistic sense, she has nothing to be jealous of. "We'll work it out, hon. Just get it to me as soon as you can."

I look away.

"Thanks, Miss Mound."

Chapter 8

"I took the night off to spend some time with my favorite girl," Dad says as I walk in the front door sopping wet. Dad's in an old blood donor t-shirt and baseball cap. Our house, all 752 square feet of it, is clean today, showing off the simplicity of our furnishings: box TV, couch, and a coffee table with a remote and coaster sitting on top. I drop my keys on the counter and begin to go through today's mail.

"Oh, hey Dad."

"I thought we could go rent a dollar movie and I'll make us some grilled cheeses."

I open the water bill, and look for the bold print *Balance Due* line. Eighty-nine dollars. I knew I should have been taking shallow baths instead of long showers. Now is not the ideal time for Dad to be taking the night off. I was too little to understand when Mom left, but I've always questioned it. Did Mom leave because Dad had no ambition whatsoever? Or does Dad have no ambition because Mom left?

"What do you think? Or do you have some big Friday night plans with Cassidy? Hot date tonight, I bet, huh?"

"No plans. I'm really tired, though. Don't know how long I'll last with a movie."

Dad takes it as a yes.

"I'll be back. I'll get us a good one before they're all picked over."

I go through more mail, and balance the checkbook while he's gone. After bills, food, and gas, this month we'll have a whoppin' seventeen extra dollars according to my calculations, but now that Dad's taking a night off, I don't know. I feel weak.

I take a shower and put on my pajamas. I want the day to go away.

Dad brings home a cheesy romance, and it goes nicely with our grilled cheese sandwiches.

Twenty minutes into it, I'm out.

I wake from a dream—one I can't remember—short of breath. My back is sweaty, but I'm freezing. I'm disoriented for just a minute. The TV is on, but black, providing a glow to the room. The box fan, still on, hums that familiar sound.

I give it a few minutes, then stretch to turn on the lamp. Dad has tucked me in with my favorite quilt. A patchwork made with my baby clothes, something that Mom made before she left. Squares the size of my hand, the quilt tells the story of once upon a time when I was a happy little girl, Dad was a happy little husband, and we were a happy little family. I smell the pink gingham square then press it against my cheek and stare at the ceiling for a while.

I roll to my side and stare down at the coffee table. My tea glass sits in a small puddle where water has rolled to my wristlet. I reach to grab the wet strap, then pull it toward me as it sloshes through more water. I slide it to the edge of the table and let it balance. Half on, half off. I stare at the wristlet until my vision blurs, fading in and out.

I finally focus, and my thoughts begin to move faster. The clock tells me it's one-thirty in the morning. Dad's snoring echoes down the hall and this with the sound of thunder creates a harmony. I wrap myself tighter in my quilt. I stare, again, at my wristlet. Ten minutes later, I act on an idea I had after I balanced the checkbook. I walk down the hallway and close Dad's door, but not all the way to where it would make noise.

Then, mascara.

Baseball cap.

Jeans, sweatshirt, and lipstick.

I walk out the front door, but move in slow motion as if I'm sneaking out. Guess I am sneaking out, but it doesn't feel wrong since it's something I have to do. The rain subsides, but the streets remain wet. I drive to the ATM down the street and decide I'm too scared to get out of the car, so I go an extra five blocks to the drive-through one.

I don't think about what I'm doing.

I just do it.

English. Checking account number. PIN. Amount: $100.

The machine spits out a receipt. *Unable to process this*

transaction. Insufficient Funds.

I try again, and I'm successful with an eighty dollar withdrawal.

There's hardly any traffic on the highway. I turn my radio on to keep me company. The streetlights reflect on the wet pavement, and everything appears extra shiny.

I can hear Dad's voice ringing in my ears, "Nothing good ever happens after midnight."

But this is different. This is work. I'm now familiar with the area, and from the interstate I see the only two things illuminated for miles, the convenience store and the casino.

I know where to park.

I know which door to enter.

Where in the world did these people come from? There are bodies everywhere. A gigantic smoke cloud hovers above, and it is the busiest I've ever seen it—two o'clock in the morning. Unbelievable.

I make my way through the crowd and pass everything from a falling down bachelorette party to an elderly couple on Hoverounds. Since I try to keep looking down at the ground, for the first time I really notice the obnoxious carpeting, a geometric pattern in brighter than bright colors. There are empty glasses left on top of ATM machines, overflowing trash cans, and very few vacant slot machines.

"Woooooooo!" A lady yells, then high-fives everyone that surrounds her. I stop to take a look—a $1250 winner according to the screen.

I start to move through the crowd again and navigate toward the poker room.

"Chelsea?!!" I hear someone call from behind me.

suit jacket. It's about to bust a button and send it into orbit. To prepare for his shift he has spread four hairs across the shiniest bald head you've ever seen.

He's still staring.

And it's making me nervous, because I already know that there's not a wait for my table.

"Give me a minute," he says rudely and turns and walks away. He whispers to another suit guy that looks my direction, and then shakes his head.

He finds a lady wearing a suit and whispers into her ear, getting closer to her than he did the guy. She shakes her head, too, and I have no idea what's going on.

My blood is pumping. I'm frozen in my stance.

Then, he waddles back to the check-in stand, scribbles something on a clipboard, and looks up at me.

"Right this way."

As I follow him through the smoke, I keep my head down and adjust my bun wad that sticks out the back of my hat. My heart is pounding. I need a chair.

He points to my assigned chair, and I can't sit down fast enough. I feel like a runner on third that has just slid in safely to home plate.

"Hey Chandra." I barely hear the dealer. I'm digging for my money.

"Hey Chandra," he says louder.

I look at him. He smiles and raises his eyebrows. He's looking straight at me.

Oh, shit, I forgot! I'm Chandra!

"Oh, hey, how's it goin'?" I hope that wasn't too obvious.

"Just wheelin' and dealin' here, Friday night in the big city."

How does he remember me? I don't remember him.

I survey the table, and I don't think I've ever played any of these people before.

While I trade my eighty dollars for some poker chips I become completely intrigued with this lady at the table who could pass for Dolly Parton's twin sister. Bleached white hair—not a strand out of place—clown-like makeup, red nails longer than her fingers, and an obvious push-up bra working double duty. Her skin is creamy white, and I take a third look just to make sure it's not really Dolly.

The old farts at my table are hypnotized by her glittery cleavage, and I'm thinking this may work to my advantage. The cowboy at the table isn't even trying to be nonchalant, he only looks away to glance at his cards. Cards, boobs. Boobs, boobs, cards. Boobs, boobs, boobs, then, not to sacrifice his boob-watching time, he tosses in his cards and tells the boobs, "I fold."

I take down the first pot, and even though it's a small win, my heart rate slightly increases. I straighten my stacks of chips, and I can feel it.

I'm in the zone.

Five hands into it, and I've got everyone figured out.

Dolly's too conservative and unsure to bluff. If she's in, I'm out.

Cowboy takes off his hat and scratches his forehead when he's got a winning hand.

Guy in red shirt is a nervous wreck. He's probably never played before.

Guy in hoodie is drunk and overconfident.

Guy on oxygen is my competition, proceed with caution.

It has all the makings of a profitable night.

Chapter 10

I get up from the table when I'm at my best, and cash in for $392 more than what I came with.

I'm relieved. I'm ecstatic.

But mostly, I'm exhausted.

I walk toward the exit and what I first believe to be a bright light shining through the glass doors reveals itself as sunlight, and I panic.

What time is it?

There's no way.

No. Way.

I turn back and look around to find a clock on the wall, but there's none.

Against the wall there's a buffet line that looks to be full of pancakes and eggs and steam with a line of white and silver-haired people waiting to fill their plates.

No way.

It's breakfast time? I don't smell breakfast. I smell cigarettes. I dig in my purse, find my phone, and learn that it's 7:15 a.m.

SHIT.

I squint at the bright beams of light as I jog to my car.

SHIT.

7:15 + 30 minute drive = 7:45.

Saturday morning.

Dad sleeps in sometimes. Not most of the time. Sometimes. Only sometimes.

SHIT. SHIT. SHIT.

I hope he—

"Hey there!"

I look over the top of a few cars to find the voice. It's bright and I can't see, but the person with the voice starts walking toward me.

"Hey!" someone says again.

It's not until he's three feet away that I realize that it's Nate. NATE. Cute Mafia Guy. *NATE.*

He takes one more step closer to me, and we're face-to-face.

Soap. He smells like soap. The cleanest smelling soap you can ever imagine. He's combed, pressed, and ready for the day. He's all morning. The parking lot goes on with its pulling in and backing out business as I stand here with Nate.

"Oh, hey." I can't look at him.

I'm gross. I slide my tongue across my teeth and feel grime. My hair under my cap stinks. My clothes are just a notch above pajamas.

"Party all night, sleep all day, huh?" He laughs.

I want to disappear but still be able to see him.

"Oh, you know . . . just making a little extra dough." That was nerdy.

He tilts his head to look under the bill of my cap.

Please don't let me have eye boogers.

He grabs at the bill of my hat and says, "You be careful out here, Chandra." He remembers my name.

I don't know my name. But he remembers it.

I'm weak. Suddenly very, very weak.

"I will. Thanks."

I want to say more to him, but I can't think of anything.

He buttons his sports coat and says, "Well, I better get in to work. See ya again soon?"

"Yeah." I look at him. "I'll be back."

"Well, good. See ya later."

Just give me a moment while I inhale your soap smell and stare at your dimples.

"Alright, see ya. Have a good day at work."

"Hey thanks. Bye." More dimples.

"Bye." I laugh.

"Bye." He laughs.

We stand still for a few seconds, then I pull my hat down on my head and walk away to look for my car. "Bye," I say one last time.

I look at my phone. 7:22.

It takes me five minutes to find my car. I'm darting between cars left and right, and I'm hoping—really hoping—that Nate doesn't have a parking lot surveillance monitor. How embarrassing. How *embarrassing*!

When I finally get to my car, I have a weird feeling because the last time I was here it was dark. I'm still weak from the whole Nate encounter, and I've got a gambler's high because of my winnings. I feel like a little girl that's been to a slumber party and stayed up all night eating cotton candy and cupcakes with sprinkles. I have to get home.

Fast.

I had to go to the store to get pads.

Cassidy is having boy problems; she needed me.

We were out of milk. (Are we out of milk?)

I was mailing bills.

Just needed some fresh air.

I had a cheer meeting at school.

We had to get sized for our cheer jackets.

I was making posters for the cross country team.

I pick the best one.

I stop on my way home and buy a gallon of milk.

As I open the door to go in the house, Dad is getting out of bed. I know this because of his bedhead and sleepy eyes when we meet.

"Hey, Dad." We pass in the living room, which takes all of five steps to walk the entire room.

Me being fully dressed this early on a Saturday morning is definitely not the norm, so I'm quick to get to the kitchen to make sure we are, indeed, out of milk.

My lucky streak is over.

Half of the gallon is still there.

"Where'd you go?" He calls over the couch.

"To get some milk."

"We have milk."

I hesitate for a second.

"It's expired." I grab the carton and start dumping it down the sink. *Chug. Chug. Chug.*

My dad sits on the couch, turns around, and squints his eyes at me.

"Are you sure? I just bought that a few days ago."

The stamped date says September 13.

"It says September 8th, Dad. Today's the 9th." I stuff the empty carton in the trash can and push it down toward the bottom, making sure the date is face-down. He walks in the kitchen, and sees me place the new carton of milk in the refrigerator. If I hadn't stopped to get the milk, I would have made it home in time. But, who knew? I had to do it. I had to have the milk as my scapegoat.

"Chelsea, are you okay?" Dad starts to make his coffee.

"Yeah, why?"

"I just noticed you haven't been hanging out with your friends as much . . . I never see Cass around anymore. You guys aren't fighting over boys or anything, are you?"

I think about his words.

He's right about Cass not being around.

"No, Dad. Don't be silly. We've both just had a lot going on, that's all." I start to make myself a bowl of Cheerios.

"Hmm. Well. Alright. Just don't let some jerk come between you two."

"Dad, we're not, seriously." I half laugh.

I kick my tennis shoes off and sit on the couch, tucking my feet underneath me.

Dad flips on the TV, and we watch the Pioneer Woman make a bacon and potato casserole, but we both know it's for entertainment purposes only—no way will we ever go through all the trouble of this recipe.

Ree Drummond.

So homemakerish.

So motherly.

So jovial.

I eat a second bowl of cheerios. Start the dishwasher. Put a load of laundry in.

And go down for a morning nap.

It's when Dad starts getting ready for his night shift that I wake up. I find my phone and realize it's already seven thirty in the evening. Two missed calls and one message from Cassidy.

Did I really sleep all day?

My room feels fuzzy. Dust particles float around in the last minutes of daylight. I roll to my back and stare at my popcorn ceiling, not knowing what to do with myself.

I stretch around under the covers, and then check the time again.

Curious what's going on in the outside world, I play her message.

"Chels? Where are ya? I was getting worried. You better hurry up; we only have an hour left . . . Call me."

What is she talking about? An hour left? There's no practice today.

I don't get it.

I get my planner and flip to September.

CAR WASH. A fundraiser.

Great.

Just great.

I call to tell her that I'm sick.

"Sick? Like stomach sick or a cold sick?" she asks.

"I think it's just allergies or something," I say. "I feel better now. I just needed some rest."

"Oh." She pauses, and then the words start spilling out of her mouth. "Chels, are you okay? Are you depressed or something? You never miss things." She pauses again. "I mean you've been so different lately."

"I'm fine." I say automatically. "I've just got a lot going on."

"Like what?"

"What do you mean, like what? School . . . cheer . . . looking for a job . . . laundry." She's clueless. Her clothes magically appear in her drawers pressed and neatly folded. She has fresh vacuum streaks in her carpet and a vase of fresh flowers on her nightstand.

"Chels, I get it. I'm not the enemy here."

"What'd you tell Ms. Mound?" I'm hopeful for a good cover.

"I didn't tell her anything. I didn't even know anything to tell." She thinks for a few seconds and adds, "That seems to be the norm these days."

"Whatever, Cassidy." I'm not in the mood for a lecture. "I don't have time for this."

"Yeah, me either."

"See ya."

"Bye." We hang up.

I sit up on my bed, grab my purse, and count my money from the night before. Wow. That really happened.

Chapter 11

I've never had $472 before. Ever. Choreography fees? Check!

I count the money three more times before I leave my bedroom. Dad is packing his sack lunch that he'll be eating around one in the morning.

"How's my favorite girl?" He says as he rolls the top of his brown bag.

"Tired."

"Tired? You've slept most the day. You must be growin' again." He's been saying this to me as long as I can remember.

"I feel like I'm fighting off a cold."

"Yeah, you sound stopped up. You better drink some orange juice."

"I will, Dad." It dawns on me. It's the casino's cigarette smoke that has wreaked havoc. I have a smoker's cough. Suddenly my lungs feel black.

"Do you have any plans tonight? Movies or anything?" He reaches to his back pocket and takes out his wallet. He offers, knowing I won't take it.

"Nah. I'm just going to stay home tonight. I don't need any money." Wait, what am I doing tonight? After hugs and a kiss on the forehead, Dad leaves for work.

I feel out of place.

I have no one to call.

I'm wide awake.

I have $472.

What's a girl to do with all of that?

"Chandra, your 1-2 no limit table is available, Chaaan-dra."

I'm standing three feet away from the guy who speaks into a microphone. I don't recognize him, but he acts all personal with everyone as if he's been doing this his whole life.

The room's crowded. I can tell it's a Saturday night. Double the cocktail waitresses, double the noise, double the smoke. The background music seems louder than usual.

I'm hopeful that Nate may still be working. A fourteen-hour shift wouldn't be totally out of the question. I sit down at my table, one in the corner. My back's against the wall, and everyone is nice and cozy. I look around the room for a suit.

"YOU SORRY SACK OF SHIT!" A player stands up and yells. He flings his cards across the table and a kid in a baseball cap—who appears to be even younger than me—starts scooping up a heap of chips. The hand's loser, a guy with five o'clock shadow, slams his chair into the table and causes the lady next to him to jump.

Immediately, there are three suit guys at our table—none of whom happen to be Nate—grabbing onto his elbows and escorting him out. The dealer holds the deck of cards in his hand and stares at the chaos until it's no longer in view.

The dealer I recognize. He looks at me, smiles for one second, then says, "Welcome to the game."

I look away at the commotion.

"Thanks."

A whole discussion starts about how the casino should just ban the guy from ever coming back . . . It's not the first time . . . He usually throws something . . . Has ruined the felt on the table by throwing a full Bloody Mary before . . .

Dad would freak if he knew I was here. Completely FREAK.

I get $200 worth of chips from the dealer. The Black Eyed Peas song, "Tonight's Gonna Be a Good Night," is playing, and I think to myself, *Let's hope so.*

I take some inconspicuous deep breaths and pop my neck to try and relax while the cards are dealt around. Meanwhile, the lunatic player's seat is being filled by the sweetest looking granny you've ever seen. She's wearing pearls and a floral dress, and I'd place her as a Sunday school teacher before a poker player.

Tonight's the night!
Let's live it up!

The Black Eyed Peas are encouraging me to bet. I look at my cards, jack/queen, and take another deep breath.

I call the first bet. I feel at home. Here it goes.

Everyone stays, and the pot is looking to be a good

one.

The community cards are dealt, and my heart about beats through my chest when two more queens come up. I'm short of breath.

Calm down, don't blow this. I tell my brain.

My hands don't get the message. They're shaking worse than the granny's at the table, only her shaky hands probably have something to do with meds.

The bet's to me.

I'm a nervous freakin' wreck.

I sound like a teenage boy going through puberty when I ask, "What's the limit?"

Everyone laughs.

The dealer explains, "You're at a no-limit table, Miss. You can bet every chip in your stack if you want."

I feel my face turn red.

I look at the cards again to make sure the three queens are still there.

The pot is huge.

I need a new pair of jeans . . . and boots.

I remember the phrase from TV, and say, "I'm all in."

It's an out-of-body experience.

The dealer cocks his head and raises his eyebrows like, are you sure about this? "Little lady's all in." He scoots my chips to the middle of the table and stacks and counts. "$200 to call."

Three of them exhale, making a *sshhh* noise. They stare me down as if I'm disrupting their mojo.

My brain repeatedly asks, Did I really just throw in $200 for one bet?

People are shifting in their chairs.

Sweet, granny Sunday school teacher has already

folded—out of turn, at that.

However, the rest aren't scared.

Five.

People.

Call.

Me.

And there's $1000 in the middle up for grabs.

My pores open and release beads of sweat.

My vision blurs. Green table felt, colored poker chips, and the dealer's hands blend together and look like a melting photograph.

Vomit percolates in my pipes. This can't be happening. Don't pass out.

$1000 in the middle. A thousand freakin' dollars in the middle!

One opponent stands. One clasps his hands above his head, tilts his head back, and exhales toward the ceiling looking for a poker God, I assume.

Are they trying to bully me? Are they all in cahoots?

Surely $1000 pots don't happen on a regular basis. This is incredible.

I realize that not one of them has looked at me since my bet. They can't make eye contact with me. That's a good thing.

My thumbnail finds my teeth and I go to town.

Workers start gathering at our table and whisper to themselves.

Nate's here.

Shit, not now.

Nate's here?

I'm every emotion all at once to the hundredth degree. It's like flicking a spinner and wondering what the hell it's going to land on, but it's taking five minutes in slow motion to do so.

What cards do these people hold in their hands?

The river. The last card of the hand gives me a full house. Good enough?

Chapter 12

The dealing is over. Everyone checks, no more betting, then three of the players reveal their hands. One player turns his face down; he knows he's not a winner.

My eyes and brain connect intensively. I can't see their hands fast enough. Straight. Straight. Two pair; he didn't make his full house.

I smile.

I laugh.

I'm euphorically dizzy.

I'm embarrassed by the mound of chips that are about to be pushed my way. The mound is HUGE.

The dealer asks, "Do you want to color up?"

I make eye contact with him. He interprets my blank stare as "I have no idea what the hell you're talking about," so he automatically starts trading my low denomination chips for larger ones. He scoops up the reds and whites and throws out some blacks.

Blacks are $100.

I have ten of them.

Ten blacks.

Ten.

Blacks.

I check them.

I recount them.

I protect them with my hand.

It's when I start to feel pain that I realize I'm chewing the inside of my bottom lip in a cannibal-like manner.

Can this be real?!

I am in no way present in the galaxy in which we live when the dealer asks me to check or fold the next hand. I can't speak. I throw my cards back in without even looking at them.

Calm down, Chelsea. Deep breaths. Neck rolls. Sit on your hands.

After four hands and still no composure, I excuse myself to the restroom. The norm is to leave your chips on the table to hold your seat. I take my blacks, drop them in my purse, and leave the rest. I string my purse crossways over my chest, and guard it as if it contains Donald Trump's checkbook.

When I walk through the crowd I feel like I have some big secret.

They don't know what I know.

I have over $1000 in my purse.

They don't know this about me.

Should I go home? Order a beer? Find a karaoke bar? Shop for clothes? Or maybe it's time to call Cassidy and tell her everything.

I don't know what to do with myself and this secret of $1000. I regroup in a bathroom stall where I take out my chips, hold them in my hands, and examine each of them, one at a time.

Cherokee Casino. Smooth, black, and worn.

Stacked neatly, I cup them in the palm of my hand, and use my other index finger to move them from one slanted direction to the other. 100, 200, 300, 400, 500, 600, 700, 800, 900, 1000.

Yes, indeed, they are all here.

I have $1000. I have a *thousand* dollars.

I place them back in my purse. Along with my cash and the chips back on the table, I'm at about $1300, something I've never had in my life.

Ten minutes later and I still can't restore my composure. An entire bottle of Valium couldn't contain my nerves right now and I decide to, as Kenny Rogers would suggest, "know when to run." When I return to the table I sit politely through three hands and throw my cards back in each time without any betting at all. I look around for the spectator group that Nate was a part of. They're gone.

I stand and start to gather my chips. The players freak.

Even Sunday school teacher Grandma chimes in, and she wasn't even part of the big hand. Her wrinkled hand with protruding veins points right at me as she scolds.

"You can't leave with all their money. This game just got started! Sit down little miss!" She points back down at my chair.

I laugh nervously.

"I can't. I've got to get to work. Sorry."

"Work?! Who needs to go to work after a win like that?!" A grizzly mountain guy holding his beer at the neck says to everyone at the table but me.

My response is not with words, it's with action. I get the HELL out of there. These people hate me. My purse holds their wages.

Coincidentally (or not?), Nate is there as I exit the poker room. I jump when he comes from nowhere and places his arm on my shoulder.

"So, you taking it home?"

I just look at him.

"The money, your big win, are you getting outta here with it? They didn't get it back, did they?"

"Oh, yeah. I'm out of here. It's all right here comin' home with mama." I pat my purse and think how stupid that sounded. *Mama?!* I hope he doesn't think I have kids.

"Do you need someone to walk you out?"

Is he hitting on me? Come to mama.

"All that money you got. I'd hate someone to follow you out. I can grab a guard to get you out to your car if you want."

Darn. Not hitting on me.

"Oh, I'll be fine. I'm a fast runner." I get stupider with each sentence.

He laughs.

I laugh back.

Awk-ward.

"Alrighty then, we'll see ya again, Chandra."

I look at my watch to speed things along.

"Yeah. Yeah, I'll see you soon."

"Alright, Ms. Chandra. Don't be hoppin' on a plane to Vegas for a poker tournament anytime soon. Well, without me, that is."

I laugh, yet again, "I won't."

I walk out of the poker room and head for the exit. Everything's fuzzy in my head. Nate. Win. Nate. Win. WIN. I won. Nate.

I'm into the parking lot in my cloud of Nate and winning when a car pulls up right next to me. A tinted window lowers, and someone in the vehicle turns down the loud bass sound of the hip-hop music.

"Heeyyy little lady, you want to be a winner tonight?" A scruffy guy in a cocked Yankees cap hangs his elbow out the window. I don't make eye contact. My pace quickens to a trot because my car is still far away.

I hear a can of something pop open, and some laughing. I glance out of the corner of my eye; it's a car full of guys.

"Hellll yeah, she wants to be a winner tonight!" A voice from the backseat says, and they all start high fiving.

I walk even faster. The car moves at my speed.

I move my purse strap over my head across my chest and start a jog.

"Dammmmmmn, girl, we ain't gonna steal your money. We just wanna chat."

Another one hollers out.

"Girl, we don't want your money." They all high five again. I cut through the aisle of cars to get on the other row, even though my car's the opposite direction. I slow to a jog. The silver, beat-up, four-door speeds up and whips around, and they're beside me, once again.

I get my phone out and act like I'm calling someone, knowing I can't call anyone at all.

This time I get a look at the driver, a guy with black hair and a black mustache, a red bandana tied around his forehead. He says, "Oh, baby, who you callin'? 911?" He stops the car and shifts to park. The passenger car door opens and a couple of them pile out. One falls, and they all crack up.

I dart back to the other row, and they're still laughing over the fall. I'm trying not to look, but I'm looking. My eyes move, my neck stays stiff.

While I'm jogging I realize I can't scream. I can't make a scene. I can't rely on security or police, because I'm Chandra. A guy that I didn't see gets out of the car jumps from out between two cars right in front of me. He reaches to grab my arm; he misses. He tries again; he gets my wrist.

Through my teeth I say, "Let go of me." I jerk my arm back, but he's got a tight hold.

"Now why you playin' hard to get, baby?"

I keep pulling my arm.

"Get the hell away from me!"

"We just want to play, baby. You lose all your money at the casino tonight, baby? Is that why you in a bad mood?"

His friends continue to laugh; one is laughing belly down over the hood of the car.

"Leave me the hell alone!" I jerk back again. My vision blurs because my eyes are full of water.

"Oh, baby. We got money if that's what you're upset about."

I hear more of them coming. Then, he sees something coming behind me and drops my wrist and runs to the car.

"Let's go!" He yells to his posse, and they manage to pile back in, shut the car doors, and speed off. Their bass is turned louder than even before, and they screech around the parking lot until they're gone.

What I thought was more of them end up being a security guard on a bicycle and Nate running behind him. The guard pulls right up, balances with one leg on the ground, and holds his bike handle with one hand, his gun with the other.

"Are you okay?" His yellow security shirt is a blur, and his question is the go ahead for me to start bawling.

Nate reaches us; the security guy gets off his bike and kicks the kickstand.

After Nate puts his arm around me, he steps back and starts looking for injuries.

"Did they hurt you? Did they steal your money? What'd they say?"

I don't know which question to answer first.

"I'm okay." I'm shaking horribly. I'm trying to contain the tears. "I'm okay, really."

The security guard pulls out his walkie-talkie when he says, "Let's call the police and make a police report."

Shit.

"No, NO, really, I'm okay. Really, I'm okay, I promise."

He's not listening. He's pulling out more stuff that looks to be communication equipment.

"Don't call the cops, please. It was nothing, I swear."

Nate intervenes, "Chandra, we're calling them."

"No, please. Please don't call them. I'm fine; they didn't even do anything. They were just playing around, is all." I start walking toward my car.

His voice gets louder, not with anger, but because I'm getting father away.

"Chandra, come back. Are you okay?" He tries to catch up with me. "Are you sure you're okay? Won't you come back in and go sit in the office with me for a few minutes? I don't think you should be getting in your car right now." He hollers back at the guard to forget the call to the cops, and the security guard complies with a, "You sure?"

The guard backs off and Nate catches up to me, then

stretches out his arm to hand me his business card.

"If you ever need me," he says. "I mean if you ever get into trouble."

Without words, I take it.

Chapter 13

The next morning I shake off the thought of those bad guys as I tuck my money—every bit of it—deep into my purse before I head to the mall. I like the idea of going to the mall and actually having money to spend. I've been a mall tagalong with Cassidy since sixth grade when her mom would drop us off for a couple of hours. Cass would try on clothes, buy outfits, sample perfumes, and look at shoes while I sat off to the side, smiling and telling her how cute she was.

Today it's my turn.

It's a whole different experience, this mall thing, when there's money in the purse. When I walk in, it's a skin care kiosk I stop at first. The guy squirts some lotion into my palm and goes into his spiel about it being European and having all natural ingredients . . . there's nothing on the market like it. He tells me I have pretty hands then starts showing me "packages" available for purchase. I lose interest, but walk away smelling the top of my hand and smiling at the fact that I *could* buy one of those packages if

I wanted. I have the money.

I go to the big department store and pass through the makeup counters then find my way to the shoes. Fall boots. Tall ones, short ones, suede, and leather. I find a gorgeous black pair with a zipper all the way down the back and flip them over to check the price. $279.

I meander around and settle on a trendy, tan suede pair, and sit down to try them on. $174 dollars seems like a bargain after checking prices and comparing. The salesman shows up to help me, a guy with white hair spending his golden years passing out hose footies. But I get it—the bills, the insurance, the need for basic things like food and electricity. This gets me to thinking . . . I wonder if they get commission and if Dad would do better here than the convenience store.

He asks, "Can I help you?" in a robotic tone.

I ask for my size, and he disappears in the back.

I can't remember anyone ever asking if they could "help me." Yes, it *is* just grabbing a pair of boots. But he *is* helping me.

He brings out my boots, and I slip them on and walk to the mirror. I've seen Cassidy do this a million times so I know this is what you're supposed to do when you go out shoe shopping. I look down at the reflection and smile because they are just that fabulous. New boots. For me! I take a few seconds to stare down at the boots before I slip them off.

"I'll take them," I say excitedly. He wraps them back in tissue, tucks them safely into the long box and walks to the register. While he rings me up, he looks at his watch twice—counting down the minutes, I'm sure, until he walks out the door to forget about smelly feet, until the next time.

Skinny jeans and leggings are a must with new boots, and I find the perfect store for those. In the dressing room I peek my head out and ask the clerk if I can pull out my boots to see how they look with the jeans.

"No problem," she says. She swings a flannel shirt over the top of my door, and asks if I'd like to try it with the jeans. I feel like royalty at this point.

"Sure," I reply, and I can't pay for the whole ensemble fast enough.

The shopping gives me hunger pangs, and I start making my way toward food, but first I get sidetracked with accessory purchases: bracelets, earrings, and a couple of to-die-for chunky scarves. I throw in a bottle of new nail polish at the last minute.

It's usually a ninety-nine cent corn dog and a water to go, but today I wander around the food court and decide to get the most expensive gyro on the menu, along with potato chips, a large Dr. Pepper, and a chocolate chip cookie for dessert. Twelve bucks. Which is next to nothing compared to the wad of cash I have deep in my purse. I even add a dollar to the guy's tip jar.

I take a deep breath in. I *love* this new position I'm in. Money . . . Nate . . . poker . . . it's as if I've stepped away from my old shell and entered into something brand new.

The tables are crowded with hustle and bustle so when I sit down to eat I crowd my bags close to me, around my feet. I've never had bags! I've had *a* bag. But never, ever, in my whole entire life have I had *bags*. I stare at my food tray a few seconds before I begin eating because I don't ever want to forget what this feels like, this first experience of luxury I'm having.

Chapter 14

Monday morning before school, I go to Miss Mound's classroom to pay all the money that's due.

She's watching *Good Morning America* and drinking coffee from a mug tattooed with bright red lipstick.

"Hi, Chelsea. Good morning." She only looks up for a second, then her eyes return to the live story on dog parks in America, the dos and don'ts.

"Good morning, Miss Mound. I have my money for you." I hand her a cashier's check that I'd bought at the convenience store. She looks at it, and her eyebrows show me she's puzzled it's not a personal check. She flips it over and looks at the back, then looks at the front again.

I stand and wait.

She looks at me, then back at the check.

"Okay, hon. Thanks." She's back in dog park land, and I slip out.

Slipping out in my new designer boots is so much better than slipping out in worn flats. AND my cheer fees are caught up. Is this what it's like to be normal?

I do everything in my power to avoid Cassidy until practice. Since I haven't returned any of her calls, I need to figure out my answers to what will be her hundred questions.

Leah, this popular girl in my third hour, comments on my boots.

"Cute boots!" she says. "I haven't seen those before."

"Thanks," I say. "I just got them this weekend."

"They're really cute. They must've cost a fortune."

I cross my legs and position my feet for her to get an even better look.

She looks again.

I smile again.

And this is the new me.

Confident. Worry-free. All bills paid.

I make it through the day with no Cassidy encounter, and I'm convinced I'm perfectly fine without her. But my luck runs out when I walk into the locker room after school, and she's the only other one in there. At first we just do our own thing. I'm putting away my books, pulling out my change of clothes, and she's doing the same. There's uncomfortable silence and lots of it.

My boots are the icebreaker. She says, "When did you get new boots?"

I look at them as if I've forgotten.

"Oh, these? Over the weekend. They were on sale."

"Oh." She goes back to changing, and I never stop changing.

I'm out on the gym floor first, and we don't say anything else to each other at all, and I'm okay with this. While stretching, I fade into deep thought. I can't help to think that it bothers Cassidy that I have cute boots. What if I had a wardrobe like hers? If I had money and she didn't, would things be different? Would we be friends?

After practice I go to get gas, and I can't ever remember pumping more than ten bucks at one time. I stand by my tank not sure what to do with all this time it takes to fill a tank. I push my cuticles down on every finger. I throw away some granola bar wrappers and a Diet Coke can from my console. But, wait! How will I know when the tank is full? Does it spill out the sides? I jump toward the gas tank and squeeze to release the nozzle. Think this through. Around me, there's no one but a stressed out mom pumping gas while her crying toddler tries to escape from his car seat. She's multitasking in heels, hose, and a khaki suit—on her cell—trying to entertain her baby with peek-a-boo through the window. Her hands are not on the gas nozzle, so I watch to see what happens.

The kid screams louder, chucks his binky though the half-opened car window, and Mom trots a few steps from the car and places her free hand over her open ear in attempt to finish the phone call. Kid still screaming.

I wait and watch.

Her gas nozzle pops down on its own. Mom walks back over to return the nozzle. So that's how.

I'm good to go. I squeeze and click. I'm fueling this baby up to the max. Full. Tank. Yes, I'm purchasing a *full tank* of gas on this glorious late afternoon. I could drive to Dallas on a full tank. I could drive to the lake. Or Branson, Missouri, probably. A full tank could take me a lot of places, yes. Liberating, this full tank of gas thing. I push away the thought of driving the country to find my mother. Those thoughts that consumed me as a child are now just sporadic and senseless.

Paying with a $100 bill and getting back some change only sweetens the deal, and when I get back in the car and turn on the ignition, the gas needle pops over to the F. Wow. It's full, alright. My tank is in post-pump shock.

I roll down the windows as I pull away from the gas station, then pull out Nate's business card for the thousandth time today. NATE BRADLEY, in bold font. CASINO FLOOR OPERATION EXECUTIVE, in even bolder font. You can look at this business card and tell he's hot for God's sake. I smell the card—that men's cologne hotness smell—and stick it back in the safest part of my purse, the zipper side pocket. I pull it back out three minutes later.

I drive with one hand, hit mute, and dial with the other.

I just want to hear what his message sounds like. He'll never know it's me. He's probably sleeping before his night shift. There's no way on earth that he'll ever figure out it's me. There's no way.

Driving faster, heart racing, I listen.

I double check the mute button. It's muted.

Rinnnng. Rinnnng. Rinnnng.

I'm right. Thank God.

"You've reached the voice mailbox of 405-6 . . ." It's the automated one. I hang up quickly. Gosh, that was stupid. A weird number that will be on his phone now, and I didn't even get to hear his voice.

Ten minutes later, I'm driving around with no particular destination, wind in my hair, when my phone rings. I go to answer, knowing it's Dad, then find out it's not when I see the number. I look at the road, my phone, the road, and my phone again before it registers that Nate is calling my phone back. What the HELL have I done now?

I don't answer, of course. I stick it under my purse so it rings less loudly.

I drive mindlessly. I look up to see a CVS not remembering when I turned this direction.

It stops ringing. I pull out my phone.

A MESSAGE.

Play messages. Play messages faster.

HOLY mother of ALL MESSAGES! A message from Nate Bradley on my phone! How could this be?!

"Hey, Chandra, this is Nate. I saw that you called, but didn't leave a message . . . just making sure you're okay. Give me a holler."

HE KNOWS IT WAS ME OH MY GOD I'M SO EMBARRASSED HOW DID HE KNOW IT WAS ME and GIVE HIM A HOLLER?!!! I toss the phone into the passenger seat and roll up my windows.

My hands get a little shaky as I drive around and fantasize about what it would be like to go out on a date with Nate. I bet he's romantic. No, I *know* he's romantic. Like a scene in a movie, I picture us at a table for two in a fancy restaurant. Candlelight and good music. Both dressed for the occasion. My hair is pulled up, in a stylish-messy kind of way; he's extra cute with starch and those dimples of his. I get lost in this daydream, and it consumes my thoughts for a good while . . . I'm sure he's the type to bring his date fresh flowers. I bet he opens doors like a gentleman and even pulls out chairs, too. Where does he live? A house? A condo downtown? Apartment? And what does he drive? A sports car? Truck?

I wonder about his family, his past relationships, and where he comes from. I think about what it would be like to date Nate Bradley.

Chapter 15

An entire week goes by before I decide to show my face in the poker room again, although it's consumed my every thought. At cheer practice I can't even get through one routine without thinking about poker strategies. A mall trip, fees, and bills, and I find myself once again in need of some blowin' and goin' money. There are other casinos, yes, but I'm not willing to give up this walk-in-without-being-questioned status I have here at the Cherokee.

Should I see Nate, I have a plan. Something that took me countless hours to finalize.

When I open the doors to the ringing of slot machines, I think, *Aaaagh, it's good to be home*. Although the air is smoky, I take a big breath and hold it for a while. I go to the restroom to check myself in the mirror and make sure the cutest outfit I've ever owned is still intact. A short skirt and shiny tank, and my trendy cowboy boots—the sum equivalent of three electric bills. There's no dire need, but I apply one more coat of lipstick onto my already perfectly lined lips.

I notice something new, has it always been there? A restaurant tucked away in the corner of the casino, Legends Sports Bar and Grill. I nose around and walk to the hostess stand. The place is empty except for a couple watching a hockey game. I figure if I fill my stomach now I'll be able to stay on the poker table longer. And I smell onion rings.

A chick in a referee shirt and extremely short shorts— if there are any even under there—takes me to a red pleather booth and hands me a menu. I'm a little nervous, stepping out of my poker room bubble, but I intend to pull this off like a regular. I slide in and look around at the million flat screens that will keep me company.

"Your waitress will be right with you." The hostess turns around then blows a whistle that's hanging from her neck. I flinch, and this is the obvious signal that there's a new customer that's just been seated. I prop up my menu and look at my greasy selections. Dad would love this place, and I think of him when I see bacon cheeseburger on the menu. It has all the trimmings, much different from the dollar menu he's used to.

In an effort to save funds for the poker table, I decide on just a side of onion rings and Diet Coke. About eight bucks plus tip, leaving me fifty-seven dollars to play on. That should do.

I don't think my waitress got the whistle message, because it takes at least five minutes for her to show up. She moseys to my table, obviously not realizing that I have some money to win over at the poker table and I don't have all day. When she walks up, I'm immediately jealous. Does Nate know this girl? She's beautiful. Her layered black hair falls perfectly from her ponytail, and her eyes are big and brown. Perfect skin too. She's thin in a fit way. "Can I get you something to drink?" She asks.

Nate loves her. I know he does.

"I'll take a Diet Coke and some onion rings." I pop my knuckles.

"Kay." She turns and moseys to the kitchen.

I turn to watch a basketball game, but I can't even tell you who's playing.

Then, it happens.

Nate walks in.

He's with two of his coworkers, I assume since they're all in suits, and they don't even wait for the hostess. They just walk to a table in the middle, no menus, and no formalities.

I scoot deeper in my booth. I feel as if my blood has drained from my body . . . that happy/weak/nervous/this-isn't-real feeling. I watch without looking, through the corner of my eye, and see Nate clasp his hands above his head and lean onto the back legs of his chair. How'd he get cuter than the last time I saw him? Is he a football or baseball kind of guy? A million questions pop around in my head. The guys are laughing, and he points to a screen and shakes his head. Just guys talking sports. Just guys, *being cute*, talking sports.

The beautiful waitress appears from the kitchen with four drinks on her tray, and she heads to their table first. Are you kidding me? They didn't even get the whistle blown, much less place an order, and they already have drinks on their table.

Nate has tea. He comes down for a drink, then returns to his leaning-back position. I watch to see if his eyes follow the waitress, and they don't. She starts heading my way, my lone Diet Coke on the tray. I'm a loner. GEESH! I'm a loner!

I start sending telepathic messages to Nate. Double-time. Please don't look this way. Please don't look this way. Please don't look this way. Please don't look this way . . .

The waitress gives me my drink. And, that's when he sees me.

He takes a double take to make sure it's me then stands up to finish his conversation. He walks toward me as he turns for one final laugh with the guys, then grabs for his tea and heads my way. He knows I'm here. I know he's here. He knows I know he's here, but I act like I don't know anyway. I dig in my purse.

"Hey Chandra, long time no see." He slides into my booth, opposite of me.

I look up and fake my shock.

"Oh, hey."

He looks good. Work suit with conservative plaid tie, and starched, pale yellow shirt.

"So you just call me then don't come around for a while?" He says in a flirty kind of way.

I laugh and look away.

"Oh yeah, sorry about that." I'm prepared. "I had called to see if there was a waiting list in the poker room because I was limited on time one day. I only had time for a few hands and thought you would know if there was an open table or not. Sorry, I shouldn't have bothered you." I finally look at him.

"Oh, well you got me all excited. I thought you were just calling me to talk to me or something. Like ask me out or something."

Thank God for the interruption when the waitress walks up, although I feel like I'm twelve years old when she sets down the onion rings. I should have ordered something more mature. Salmon. Bruschetta. Prime Rib. Gosh, anything but onion rings. The waitress asks if I need anything else, and I shake my head no so I don't have to speak. She walks off, and we're alone once again.

Nate grabs an onion ring off the mountain, and says, "What were we talking about again?" He answers for me. "Oh yeah, you called me because you wanted to ask me out on a date." He's chompin' away, and he feels right at home. He smiles as he opens the ketchup and pours some on the side of the plate.

"Ummm, no."

He dunks his half-eaten onion ring into the ketchup, something that would typically gross me out—double dipping—but it doesn't bother me.

"What? You don't want to go out with me?" He grabs his heart and pretends he's crushed. But he knows better.

I start eating.

"Well, I didn't say that either." I feel fuzzy.

He takes a drink.

"Oh, so you are asking me out? Sure, I'd love to." Dimples. I see nothing but dimples.

Chapter 16

Okay. So it's not a good night in the poker room, and after three hours I go home with an extra fourteen dollars in my purse. My concentration was a little off to say the least (duh, Nate). Well, that and the extra possessive woman who thought I was trying to steal her truck driver husband (think Dog the Bounty Hunter and wife) didn't help. Did she really think I was interested in him?

I walk out to my car still wondering how the hell I'm going to pull off a date with Nate. He's just too cute to pass up. *Chandra, your name is Chandra.* I tell myself until I'm convinced.

I continue my daydreaming on the drive home about how this date will actually go down. Will he try to kiss me? What will I order? Will he ask me where I work? I've got a lot of planning to do. Or, Chandra has a lot of planning to do, rather. I take one hand off the wheel to rub my palm on my temple to discourage the headache that's building intensity. I turn off the radio.

I'm stupid.

I'm stupid for thinking I can pull this off.

How did I let myself get sidetracked? I'm so damn stupid.

I bet he wears a starched shirt. Good grief, I love him in starch.

I have no one to tell about Nate, and I imagine what Cassidy would have to say about it if she knew where he worked. Probably something like, "He's cute? Just go up and say 'Heeeyy. How 'bout you and I start workin' on a full house?'" or "I bet you're an expert on seven-card STUD, huh?" I laugh to myself, but I feel like crying because I miss her.

I walk in the door to find Dad flipping through the channels. He's scruffy. Sweat pants, flannel, stubbles on his face.

"There's my girl," he turns off the TV. "Are you hungry?"

Being that a single onion ring is the only solid my stomach's received for about eight hours, I reply, "Starving."

"Oh, I figured you and Cass were out on the town having a nice lunch or something."

"Huh-uh."

"So what have you been up to all day?"

I hesitate.

"Oh, just some cheer stuff up at school. I had to go to the library, too." I imagine my nose growing like Pinocchio's.

"Do we owe any money on your uniform? I should have some overtime on the next check, at least an extra forty bucks or so."

Dad is clueless at the cost of things these days.

Especially cheer things.

"Don't worry about it, Dad, I think we're doing a fundraiser sometime soon." I feel my nose grow longer. Dad would die if he knew those things are about 250 bucks a pop.

"Mac and cheese?" I change the subject.

After dinner I decide to call Cassidy, and thirty minutes later we're on our way to the movies. Since things are a little tense between us, I decide to tell her a teeny, tiny bit about what's going on.

"You are shitting me. Is that how you got your new boots?"

"Well, kinda. I guess." I second-guess myself for telling her. "Cass you can't tell ANYONE. I mean technically it's against the law, you know that, right?"

"I can't believe this. My best friend is a compulsive gambler. What the hell!" She's dramatic.

I laugh it off.

"I'm not! I've been TWICE. It's no big deal. Really. I'm not going back. But there's a really cute guy there." I tingle just mentioning him.

"Are you kidding me?!" She turns down the radio.

"His name's Nate. He works there." I decide to spill it all. "We're actually meeting up for a date next weekend."

"Are you freak-ing kidding me?" She gets all silent, processing . . . processing . . . processing.

No one has to tell me I'm stupid. I know this already.

Let the Cassidy interrogation begin.

"How old is he? Where did he go to high school? Has he ever been married? For shit's sake, does he have kids? Does he live by himself?" As expected, the questions go on . . . and on . . . and on.

I love Cass. Of course. Almost by default, like you have to love a sister because she's your sister. But sometimes I want her to go away because no matter how close we are, she will NEVER understand how I feel or what it's like to be me.

I answer her questions, like a good sister, and assure her that I'll be careful.

As we watch the movie, I wish it were Nate sitting beside me instead of Cass. And again, I'm a million miles away.

Chapter 17

Playing hooky from school is justified when you have work to do.

Dad will receive an automated call reporting my absence, so I cover my tracks before they're even made. I open his bedroom door then knock to wake him up.

"Dad?"

He rolls over and replies in a very slow and sleepy voice.

"What's up, Chels?"

"Dad, I'm not going to school today. I have a research project I'm working on so I'll be at the library all day. The school automated thing will be calling. Didn't want it to scare you."

He barely opens his eyes and readjusts his old blanket.

"The library? Look at my smart girl." Dad makes no mention that I shouldn't be missing school.

I walk into the library and sit at an open computer in the back row but get a little sidetracked before I begin. Mothers bring their toddlers in for story time, and I start daydreaming and wondering if my mom ever brought me to hear a story. Little girls with short pigtails and ribbons, little boys with combed-over hair. All kids deserve to sit on their mother's lap and hear tales like *The Little Engine That Could* and *Brown Bear, Brown Bear*. It's a precious time for all involved, and for ten minutes I sit and observe moms tying shoes, mom and toddler selfies, and moms handing crackers to their little ones.

I swivel side to side in my chair then decide it's time to get proactive. I begin my search for jobs in the area, something I do often. I hit all the main sites, and make notes for three jobs that look like potentials. A retail job that pays commission sounds most promising, but there's something very uncomfortable about lying to people about how good they look in stuff they can't afford. High-pressure sales. Ugh. I can't seem to get too excited about a minimum wage, paid-by-the-hour job either. The pot I won the other night would be the equivalent of about seventy hours of work. It took five minutes.

I get sidetracked on a recreational gaming site, and I play poker, for fun, until almost ten in the morning. Then I realize that I could actually be learning something about the game itself.

I search: How To Win at Poker. How To Read Your Opponents. The Millionaire Poker Player. Poker Skills. A million sites with a billion articles and videos come up in my search, and I can't believe I've never thought of this before. I go to the front desk and ask for some headphones.

I walk through the library and check each aisle, making sure there's no one here, by chance, that I know. I go back to my computer and feel like I'm back here about to embark in criminal behavior.

I'm mesmerized. I spend the next five hours learning tricks about the game of poker—things I've never even thought about or even considered.

I can't believe this information is out there. The experts are incredible. Why is the whole universe not on to this? Why are people working miserable jobs when they could be sitting on a poker table making a living? How could something so available seem so untapped? I feel like a secret member of a club after I educate myself all day. I'm empowered, and my heart rate goes up just thinking about my next opportunity on the poker table.

Somehow I manage to be running late to the first football game of the year.

Simultaneously, I drive and place an oversized red bow on the top of my head. Not sure who started the big bow trend, but I look in the rearview mirror and confirm it's ridiculous. The bow is as big as a football. Why are we wearing footballs on the top of our heads? Bows. Who needs 'em?

"Daddy, Kailey said her mom makes her hair bows with a hot glue gun."

Dad looked at me. "Hair bows?"

"Yeah, those big ones with the ribbons and jewels and feathery things."

"Oh." Dad flipped the channel. He flipped some more.

"Why? Do you want hair bows?"

"Well, yeah, I guess. But I don't know how to make them."

He cranked back in his recliner. "I'm sure it can't be that hard. It's just a hair bow."

"Yeah." I knew in my head Dad couldn't make what I had in mind. He stopped on a fishing show just as they were reeling in a big one. I explained, "They're about this big, and a jewel holds them together in the middle."

He was entranced by the bass.

"Dad?"

"Oh, yeah, honey, hair bows . . . draw me a picture and I'll give it my best shot."

The parking lot fills quickly, and I inch my little car between two SUVs, one of which is halfway into my parking space too. I crack my door open to realize there's no way I'm getting out, slam my door back, then crawl to the passenger side to avoid reparking. Before I open the door, I look up to the heavens and say, "Dear God, please don't let any casino people recognize me. I'll be better. I promise. Amen." I get out of the car, tie my shoes, and run toward the field.

"You're late." Cassidy is already on my case.

"I know that." I look for Miss Mound, but she's not around.

"Let me guess. Casino?" She says just a little too loudly. I look to make sure no one heard then squint my eyes at her sending the, "What-the-hell-are-you-thinking?" message.

I go down in the splits to start stretching with the rest

of them, and keep my face down toward my knee, looking up through the corner of my eye.

Please.

Please. Please. Please. Don't let anyone recognize me.

I look down each row of bleachers as they start to fill with kids, grandparents, teenagers, and moms and dads—all dressed in red and black. An old guy in overalls makes my heart stop, but after my eyes adjust and zone in, I decide he's not a poker player.

If only this were a day game, I could wear sunglasses. The big ones. No one would be able to recognize me then. I think of a million ways to hide my face as we line up to run through and practice our halftime routine. As we wait for the music to start, I look down at my shoes and pretend my foot itches.

The music starts. A hip-hop song that's so loud it sounds like the speaker could crack any second.

"Five. Six. Sev-en. Eight." Miss Mound comes from behind us and lets her presence be known.

Like a little kid, I take the, "If-I-don't-look-they-can't-see-me" approach. I go through the entire routine without looking into the stands. But my mind spins a million ways I'll be recognized. A cocktail waitress attending her brother's game. A poker player visiting his alma mater. A truck driver pulling over for a hot dog.

I'm screwed.

I go through the motions. Then, it's time. The stands are full. The football players come out. We grab our pom-poms and do our thing on the sideline. The football players line up down the field, black jerseys, silver numbers. Number 42, Caleb Vanhoose, comes back for a drink. I notice. He takes his time and looks into the stands, and I pray he doesn't have an Uncle Charlie that knows what it means to have an inside straight. He looks at me, oddly, and I panic that somehow he's received a telepathic message that I'm a poker player.

He smiles.

Eyebrows raised, I smile back.

Cassidy's on it.

"What was that? Did you see the way he looked at you? Wow!"

"I don't think he was looking at me." I adjust my skirt and bend down to tie a shoe that doesn't need to be tied.

"Ummm, yes he was," she says.

At halftime, we run to take our places on the field. I barely smile, thinking a big smile will only draw attention. We stand there, waiting for music. We stand there longer, waiting for music. Is this really happening? Play the damn music! I frantically scan the stands, praying this isn't a bust. We are motionless, pom pons at our hips, waiting for something . . . anything to happen. I start on row one, and strain to look at every single spectator.

Row one . . . I'm safe. Row two . . . Row three . . .

I get halfway through the crowd when the music starts.

Then I see Nate.

Chapter 18

At home, I lie in bed and pull the covers over my head. I tell Dad I'm not feeling well.

A few minutes later, he brings me a bowl of chicken noodle soup and sets it on my nightstand.

"Thanks, Dad. I'm not really hungry though."

He feels my forehead.

"I'll leave it here in case you get hungry, honey. You sure you don't need me to take off work tonight?"

I rest my arm over my head. "I'm sure, Dad. I think I'm just run-down or something."

"Well, get some rest. Call me if you need me." He buttons his work vest and walks out my door.

My phone rings. Of course, it's Cassidy.

I get it over with.

"Hello."

"Where did you disappear to? I thought you just went to the bathroom."

"I did."

"Did you fall in and end up in the ocean? What the

101

hell, Chelsea? You can't just keep disappearing."

"What'd Miss Mound say?"

"Where are you, Chelsea? Answer my question!"

"I'm home."

"Miss Mound was wondering too. The whole squad was wondering." She took a deep breath, in a put-out kind of way. "You're home?"

I roll over.

"I'm in bed. I think I'm getting sick. My stomach hur—"

"Enough already!" She cuts me off. "You're not sick! What is going on with you, Chelsea?! Caleb Vanhoose asked me where you were after the game and I didn't even know what to say!"

"I saw Nate in the crowd." Caleb Vanhoose, huh?

"Who?"

"Nate. From the casino. He was with a girl."

"The casino guy? ARE YOU CRAZY? Who cares who that guy is with, Chelsea! You have no business flirting around with him anyway! Did he see you?"

"I don't think so. I hope not. He's never seen me play poker looking like a wrapped gift with that bow on my head. Hopefully he didn't recognize me."

"Chelsea, do you realize how much trouble you'd be in if you were caught? You'd go to jail, Chelsea. Or he'd go to jail. This is getting ridiculous."

We sit in silence.

I decide to appease her.

"You're right. I'm done with it. I'm done with the poker. I'm done with flirting with Nate. I'm done."

She replies, "Well good. Welcome back to reality." We sit on the line in silence for a few seconds. She breaks the silence. "Chelsea, you know if you ever need a loan that I can help you out."

I think of the stack of bills and start to cry. She has no idea.

"I do. I need a loan, Cassidy. Just fifty bucks to get me through the weekend." Tears stream down my face, and my nose starts to run. "I'm afraid we'll lose our electricity. I can't let Dad know. He has no idea how much money all this cheer stuff . . ." I cry. "I don't know why I thought I could pull this off." I can't stop crying.

Cassidy listens for a few seconds. She doesn't know what to say. Finally, she comes up with, "I'm on my way."

After a lot of tears and a little laughter, Cassidy opens up her Coach bag, and digs for her wallet. I want to stop her, but I need the money. Even if it's just Cass, I'm still humiliated.

She lays a $100 bill on my nightstand.

"I don't need that much." I sit up.

"Take it. You can pay me back after you find a job or something. It's not that big of a deal." She walks toward the door and zips up her purse.

The money sits on the nightstand.

"Thanks. This helps. A lot." I slide back down into my covers. "You have no idea how much this helps. I'll pay you back as soon as I can. I promise."

"Get well soon." She replies as she walks out the front door.

I stare at the money for a long time.

I think of a lot of things: Dad working at the convenience store, my new boots that sit in my closet, the growing stack of bills, and empty refrigerator.

I think of Nate and a girl.

I want to push any thought of Nate out of my mind, so I get up and start opening mail.

Gas. Plus late fee.

Telephone and cable. Time to stop cable service, again.

I climb back into bed.

Flip through the channels.

Look over at the $100 bill.

Flip through the channels.

And look at the money again.

Chapter 19

I'm confident Nate's not working when I pull in. He's probably sharing pizza and a pitcher of beer with his date right now, but when I walk through the doors, I look for him anyway.

It's not that crowded, for a weekend night, I think to myself. There's a country band playing in the corner—people sitting around playing slot machines while they listen to a guy trying to sound like George Strait. Key word: trying.

There's no waiting list for the poker room. A guy in a suit points me back to table seven, and in no time I'm back in business.

I join the table during a dealer change, so players are making small talk and pulling out their phones. I look around and relax knowing that 100 percent for sure there's no Nate.

For it not to be crowded, it smells extra smoky tonight. One would think that I would be building some sort of immunity to the smell of smoke . . . maybe get used to it by now . . . but I fight the urge to pull my t-shirt over my nose and mouth to serve as a filter . . . it's bad. Way bad.

I know the routine. I place my $100 on the table and wait for chips.

I'm comforted when the Sunday-school-looking teacher from the other night gets up to move next to me. She sits down, squeezes her shawl with one hand, and straightens her chips with the other. She smells unlike a typical granny; it's a clean and fresh smell. A bath spray . . . berries or something of that sort. Her smell is like an oxygen line in this smoke infestation. As she straightens her stacks, I decide that this is a woman who takes care of herself. Her hands are old, yet moisturized. Her skin is the best it could possibly be for a woman her age—milky and wrinkled, but in a beautiful way. There's no wedding ring, and this makes my mind wander. Was she married? Does she have kids that check in on her? Did her husband of a million years pass suddenly? There are players here to pay the mortgage, and there are players here for entertainment. She's here for entertainment, no question. And this hurts my heart for reasons I can't figure out. I want to be her friend. I want to make sure she has "people."

"Havin' a good night?" I ask as I nod down to her stack of chips.

She giggles. "Oh, honey. It depends what you consider a good night." She giggles again.

"It looks good to me."

"Easy come . . . easy go. You know how this game works." She punctuates, again, with a giggle.

The dealer, a tall, thin guy with a ponytail and wire rim glasses, twists to pop his back, then stretches from one side to the other. He sits down on his personal donut cushion and says, "Let's get this party started, shall we?"

A beer bottle is raised and a "Hellllll yeah!" comes from a guy in a cowboy hat that has obviously started his party hours ago.

I look at each of them. But mostly, I look at their chips. I need their chips. In a really big way.

The dealer pops his back one last time, and then shuffles the cards. He claps his hands once, shows his palms to the security cameras in the ceiling, then says, "Good luck, everyone."

I pat Granny on the back, lean over and whisper, "Watch out, boys."

"Girl power!" She whispers back.

On the opposite end of the table, an old, chunky lady with yellow hair and black roots picks up a troll doll and kisses it. She sets it back on the table next to her, and I can't help but wonder if that technique has worked for her in the past.

The cards find their way to my hands, and I get the warm fuzzies before I even take a look.

Girl power. Yes, indeed. "I raise six dollars."

Granny, to my left, folds.

My hand—a king and queen—has done it for me in the past, and I begin to study the players that have wagered to join me.

The betting makes its way around the table, but comes to a halt with the drunk guy. It's obvious that this isn't the first time the dealer has dealt with this joker. "Joe. Are you in?!"

Joe dramatically scratches his head, squints at his cards, and says (loud enough for the people at the next table to hear) "Does a bar have beer?! Hell, yeah, I'm in!" He's cracked himself up.

No one else is amused, to say the least.

Joe throws his chips in and one goes rolling over to our side of the table.

The dealer takes notice and stares down Joe.

"We'll consider that your warning, big guy."

"Warning?! Hell, what'd I do? You mean to tell me . . ." (Pause while Joe collects his thoughts.) "That a guy can't . . ." (Pause while Joe blinks slowly and . . . continues to . . . collect his thoughts.) "That a guy can't splash the pot every once in a while?"

The dealer spends no energy on this. He's moving on.

Cards are dealt. I'm in good shape. I send him a telepathic sympathy note.

Joe, I'm sorry for your misfortune of drinking too much and letting me win your money tonight.

Bets are moving around the table, and the troll doll lady catches me off guard. "I'm all in."

Where the hell did that come from?

Is she bluffing?

She picks up the troll doll and holds it next to her heart, face out.

This is . . . weird.

The troll doll is staring me down.

I clasp my hands together and take a deep breath.

I roll my head to pop my neck.

Three of a kind. Queens are what I have . . . Granny did say 'girl power' before the hand. They are queens. Queens are girls . . . I'm rationalizing every possibility to stay in this hand.

She's frozen with the troll doll. I stare her down for

thirty seconds, at least.

She pulls the troll doll from her chest, smooths its hair, and then brings it back to her chest. Bingo.

"I call." At least half the money I came with I push to the center of the table. I push thoughts of Cassidy out of my mind and convince myself that she wouldn't get it. She doesn't understand my situation. She's never had to worry about money. She'd be doing this too if she were in my position. $100 is like ten to her. I'm just earning interest on her money. She would be doing this too.

Troll doll is brought to the lady's lips, and she kisses it a few times for good luck.

What is she playing for? Does she want a new pair of hot-pink, strappy heels? A new shade of lipstick? Or is it down to the wire and she needs gas money to get to her job at the outlet mall?

Other than the drunk guy closing his eyes for a power nap, everyone at the table is ready to see the results.

The dealer says, "Let's see 'em."

I can hardly breathe. This has to be the equivalent of running a 5K. I picture Dad and me sitting in the dark eating by candlelight after they've shut off our electricity.

I'm slow to turn my cards over as I watch the lady stand, place the troll doll on her stack of chips (he's been freed), and reveal her hand.

THANK YOU. THANK YOU. THANK YOU, JESUS. It's just two pair.

Sunday school teacher gives me a pat on the back and mumbles under breath, "That's what she gets for believing in a troll doll. Those things give me the creeps."

"No kidding." I smile but can't look at the lady that I just beat. I hope it was just lipstick she was playing for.

I hope she can still get to work.

Before I can even get my chips stacked, we're on to the next hand. I finally get the nerve to look across the table, and she's tucking the troll doll away in her purse. It's as if he's being punished. He's being replaced. A bigger, better, blue-haired troll doll is placed on top of her dwindling stack of chips, then she takes a look at her cards.

When Sunday school teacher asks me to go share a plate of nachos with her I can't say no—hole in my stomach aside. There's something I like about her. Like one of those people you automatically connect with. I leave my poker chips on the table and walk across the casino to a small strip of fast food joints, a mini-version of a food court in the mall. When we make our way to the register of Taco Time she's greeted by a kid wearing a hairnet who looks, maybe fourteen.

"Hey, Miss Stella." He's a bit confused, like I've disrupted their regular routine.

Stella plops her purse on the counter and smiles.

"How's my favorite chef?" she asks. It's a one-man band, Taco Time. It appears he does the order taking, the cashiering, and the cooking too.

"Doin' okay. Doin' okay, Miss Stella."

"Good deal, Deon." She looks up at the menu, but already knows.

"The usual?" He asks, then looks at me again in confusion.

"Deon, I'm living on the edge today. Give me a large order of nachos, hon."

"Well, well . . . That poker table must be treatin' ya alright then, Miss Stella?" He punches the order into the register. "Large nach-os. Sprite today, pretty lady?"

"Yes, and one for my friend here, too."

I feel warm when she calls me her friend. Stella has that aura about her, warm and sunshiny. Her presence is comforting. We find a table and sit across from one another. She gets up to get salsa, and I wait to start eating until she gets back.

"Dig in, hon." She grabs a nacho as she sits down. "I want to help you out, Chandra."

"Help me out?" Help me out? Does she know I'm desperate for money? Does she know I'm without a mother? How does she know I need help?

She finishes chewing before speaking.

"Let me tell ya something, hon. That table. If the joker in the straw hat raises on the second round, get out. Fold without thinking. Don't ever, ever . . ." she looked me in the eyes, "stay in a hand with Jim. That is, after he's raised on the second round."

Oh, I get it now.

"Well thanks, good to know." I take a loaded nacho from the middle, one with a mound of meat and sour cream. "Anything else?"

She thinks a few seconds as she chews.

"Do you have kids?"

I giggle.

"Oh, I meant are there any other poker tips?"

"I know what you meant, hon. You have kids?"

My first thought was Dad. Well *yeah*, I have a kid.

"Nope, no kids yet."

She goes for the middle of the nacho plate too.

"Hmm. No kids, huh. How old are you?" She doesn't give me time to answer. "When I was your age I already had one and one on the way."

I laugh.

"It will be a while before kids."

We sit and enjoy our nachos together, with slot machines ringing in the background.

"So how many kids do you have?" I ask.

She pauses a minute, contemplating her answer.

"Oh, never mind them, hon."

I knew it. Stella has sadness. She has some type of sadness in her life. I knew it. So maybe that's our connection.

We sit in silence for just a few minutes as we finish eating. Ms. Stella digs in her granny-style purse and pulls out a stack of business cards wrapped with a rubber band. She pulls one from the stack and pushes it across the table with me. "Here, hon." She taps the card a couple of times. "If you ever need anything."

I read the bright pink card. STELLA'S SILVER SCISSORS - ALERATIONS AND SEWING. 4544 Bluffcreek Drive. 405-912-0909.

"Oh, thanks, but I don't ever really get any of my clothes altered."

She smiles a motherly smile.

"Not for alterations, sweetie. For just anything."

I place the card in my purse to let her know that yes, I may need her. "Thanks, Ms. Stella."

"Goodnight, doll." She leaves.

And that's where the goodness ended. When I get back to the table I don't win another single hand. The one against the troll doll is the only hand I win all night long. I didn't give drunk guy enough credit. The more he drank, the more careless I played, the more *he* won. Pathetic.

Down to my last three dollars, and I hate myself. I

should have gotten up after that first big win. I know better. I sit through three hands in total disbelief before I force myself to the door.

Although it's four o'clock in the morning, I stop and pump three dollars' worth of gas. Actually, I stop pumping at $2.99 because I'm scared to death the stupid thing will run over by two cents or something, and I don't have the extra two cents. The drive seems longer than usual. It's eerie because I'm literally the only one on the road—highway and side streets. The rest of the town is tucked in to their warm beds and not worrying about their electricity being shut off.

When I get home I make myself a cheese sandwich and eat just two bites before I go to my room, climb into bed, and curl up into fetal position. I don't want to deal with this mess.

I don't want to be me.

Chapter 20

"Chels, honey, you better get up . . . It's one thirty in the afternoon." Dad rustles my hair, and I hear him walk out.

I stretch and remember the shit creek I'm in before I even open my eyes. *Why me?*

The only thing I'm thankful for is that it's still the weekend. I can't bring myself to get out of bed. My mind wonders about ways to earn fast cash. Plasma donation. Clean someone's house. Street corner with cardboard sign of desperation. I can maybe sell some stuff. My new boots on Ebay? But it would take at least a week for that transaction.

I muster the energy to sit upright when my phone rings. The first ring sends a signal to my brain that I can't afford this phone, and I need to sell it. The second ring signals a message to actually pick it up and answer it. The number looks familiar, but I don't know who's calling.

I let out a perky "Hello," trying to fool whoever is calling into believing that I've been awake for hours.

"Hey, it's Nate."

I'm wide awake now. I stand up to prove it.

"Oh, hey . . ." I say in a way that shows no excitement. In a way that tells him that, you know, this is an everyday occurrence . . . guys calling me all the time and such.

"Are you busy?" he asks.

"Oh, no. Just getting some laundry done. You know, those Saturday afternoon chores." I move to shut my door.

"Gotta love those chores. Hey, I was wondering if you'd want to meet for dinner tonight. Something low-key . . . maybe pizza or something like that."

"Can you hold on for just a sec?" I sit down on my bed and scoot the phone under the covers to process this. Dinner? CRAP. Dinner? What happened to his girlfriend? I stand up and look in the mirror on my wall and quickly fix my hair. As if he can see me through the phone.

"Okay. I'm back." No response.

"You there? Nate?"

"Yeah, I'm here. What do you think?"

"About?"

"About meeting me for dinner tonight?"

I ask him point blank.

"Um, don't you have a girlfriend?"

He laughs.

"Have a girlfriend? Why would I be asking you out if I had a girlfriend? Nope. No girlfriend here."

"Hmm. Are you sure about that?"

He laughs again. "I'm sure, I'm sure . . . I know it's shocking that a charming guy like myself is single, but it's true. No girlfriend."

I muster up the courage.

"Well I thought I saw you with a girl one day."

"A girl?" He pauses a few seconds. "I have a twin sister, and we run around quite a bit, maybe that's who you saw." He appeases me. "Where at?"

"Uhh, I can't remember, I'm guessing it would have to be the casino." I stammer.

IT WAS JUST HIS TWIN SISTER AND HE IS SINGLE!

"Well, you're not avoiding my question, are you?" Nate gets back to business. "Dinner tonight?

"Oh yeah, sure. Sounds fun."

"Cool. Would you rather me pick you up or do you want to meet?"

"Meeting sounds good. I've seen what can happen on pick-up dates. I watch *48 Hours*, you know."

He laughs. A really cute laugh, I must say, then replies, "I wouldn't sink you to the bottom of the lake on the first date, silly. That's like, third date stuff."

"Ha. Ha. Very funny."

We decide to meet at an old Italian restaurant downtown, one I've never been to, one he goes to all the time. For five minutes I'm completely unaware of my financial "situation." Until I hang up and remember my car has no gas.

I open my door and walk into the living room. My dad is flipping the channels about to go down for his before-work nap when he looks up to acknowledge me.

"Heeeey, Sleeping Beauty. All that sleep just makes you more and more gorgeous, kiddo. I better clean my gun so I can get ready to fight off all the boys that are going to be knockin' down my door."

"That's hilarious, Dad."

Wait a minute.
Gun.
Dad's gun.
Gun is valuable.
Gun can be pawned.
No, that's ridiculous.
I could never do that.
That's what desperate drug users do.
I could never do that.

Chapter 21

I wait for Dad to roll over on the couch and enter the REM state of sleep before I go back and sneak into his closet with a black garbage sack. It's in the corner, behind his flannels, and I pray it's not loaded because the thought freaks me out.

I grab a throw blanket off his bed and tuck it in around the rifle, then peek down the hallway to make sure Dad's still out (although I know he'll be out for at least two hours).

It's a go.

I feel like a criminal.

I am a criminal.

Is it considered stealing if it comes from your own house?

Surely not.

Ever-so-quietly, I sneak out the front door and choose to leave the door open since I'll be right back.

I'm eighty-five percent sure there's a pawn shop next to this buffet restaurant that I've eaten at before. Before now, I've never given much thought about pawn shops, and basically all I know is that they give you money for items that you can come back and get.

I'm extra attentive to the speed limit signs because getting pulled over with a gun in a trash bag would not be a good thing. My hands are at ten and two on the wheel, and I'm using my turn signal like never before.

It's about five minutes from my house, and approaching the major intersection I squint to see the shop on the corner of the strip mall. Bars are in the windows. They buy gold and silver. The sign says All-American PAWN Shop. I wonder what this has to do with being American. I pull around the parking lot once. It's disgusting. Trash, excessive oil spillage from broken-down cars, and faded yellow lines giving people a vague idea of where to park. I feel sketchy already.

I find the closest parking space possible, one reserved with two old Happy Meal boxes that have been run over a time or two. I sit in my car for just a few minutes to observe the people going in and out of this place. A young couple, about my age, gets out of their beater—a faded chalky red color—and the dad pulls an infant carrier with a baby from the backseat. The baby is asleep. What are they here to hock? Trading a necklace for diapers wouldn't be a bad thing at all. You gotta do what you gotta do.

I sit for a while longer, glancing in my rearview mirror a couple of times.

The gun isn't going to walk in and pawn itself, so I get out of the car and open the back door. Without opening the bag I feel around to make sure I grab the gun barrel-down. Am I really doing this?

The sidewalk is uneven so I walk extra slowly and

119

extra carefully.

A gun.

I'm carrying a gun for God's sake.

As I push through the door a buzzer rings. It's a department store on a smaller scale. An electronics department showcases flat screen TVs, and they're all on the same channel showing the evening news. I pass through kitchen appliances then walk back to the counter, and I notice the security monitors showing about nine angles of the parking lot before I even notice the worker.

"Whatcha got?" He looks down at my bag.

My response is delayed because I'm incredibly distracted by the handgun holstered to his hip, partly concealed by his belly fat. Good grief—could a hiccup trigger that gun?

"Uhh," is all I can come up with. I reveal the rifle and place it on the counter. I smell power tools and electronics with a hint of men's cologne. Cheap cologne.

"Uh huh . . . You've gotcha an old twenty-two, do ya?" I begin to shake when he opens it up and starts making all those loud gun-cocking noises.

"Yeah."

"What, you givin' up deer hunting this year?" He cracks himself up.

I fake laugh then respond, "Yeah."

He pulls out a blank order form and starts filling out information about the gun in all capital letters . . . serial number and description. There's a box with a dollar sign showing that sixty dollars is the principle amount of the loan. I don't bother with reading the volume's worth of fine print because I'll be back by tomorrow to retrieve it. He points to a place for me to write my information and sign at the bottom. I decide—on the fly—that I'll give all correct information, and it's a good thing I do because he asks for my driver's license.

It takes no time for him to verify my information and pull three twenties from the cash drawer. And boom. I'm pulling out with sixty bucks.

Chapter 22

I pump ten dollars' worth of gas into my tank knowing that will be plenty, round trip, for the Italian restaurant downtown. When I get home, Dad's in the exact position he was when I left: hands clasped behind his head, knees bent, as if he fell asleep in the middle of a sit up.

I try not to make any noise. I go back to my room and begin to regroup. My bed is unmade. My nightstand is cluttered with papers. I scoot my covers to the end of the bed and start making stacks. Graded school assignments. Notes and fliers from school. Bills. Checking account statements.

I've got fifty bucks. Dad gets paid in four days. I'll go by and pay ten dollars toward the electric bill and beg them not to turn it off. It's worked before, but it all depends on who's working and what kind of a mood they're in. The whole thing is humiliating. But so is going to school with wet hair if our electric was to get cut off. I take all my stacks and compile them back to one stack and set it back on my nightstand.

I begin to flip through my closet and try on clothes. Thirty minutes and a mound of clothes later, I decide on old jeans and a coral button-down shirt that I can tie at the waist. However, that night, I leave in a short, black cotton dress, barelegged with my boots.

As I drive downtown, I look forward. Forward. Forward. Forward. I do everything I can to avoid looking over and making eye contact with any driver on the street. For Nate to see me driving to our date would be so . . . awkward. I tell myself he's probably coming from a different direction, but I still feel like such a goob.

Downtown is packed. Teenagers, families, old people . . . it's a potpourri of Okies down here. I find the restaurant and pull into the parking lot across the street. A lot attendant holds a sign, but he's turned around talking to a group of women wearing conference badges, so I can't read what the sign says. I find a space, and take a few deep breaths.

When I get out of the car, it takes effort to walk. I didn't think I'd be this nervous. I'm about to cross the street when I see the lot attendant coming after me. He's hollering, "Hey! Miss!"

From the corner of my eye, I see Nate walk out of the restaurant.

The attendant catches up to me, and I realize why he's chased me down. The sign says parking is eight dollars.

EIGHT DOLLARS.

I smile at the man (Nate's watching), and get a ten from my purse. The attendant, a guy in his sixties, makes change. I don't have time to process this expense or the impact it will have on my financial situation. I cross the street.

Nate laughs.

"Trying to slide by the ol' parking lot guy, are ya?"

I feel my cheeks flush red.

"Oh, no. I didn't see his sign, that's all."

"Yeah, that's what all the parking lot bandits say."

I laugh.

"I'm not a parking lot bandit."

Nate opens the door for me, and we enter the restaurant.

It's a cozy little place. Dim lights. Round tables with red checkered tablecloths. Couples sharing bottles of wine. The smell of bread hangs in the air. Although it's a relaxing atmosphere, my hands begin to shake.

Nate makes his way to the hostess stand, and I follow behind. The hostess (the only one in this joint that seems to be my age) tells Nate it will be a twenty-minute wait.

"That's fine. We'll just wait in the bar," he responds. He takes my hand and pulls me toward a cramped row of barstools where I stand behind him, still holding his hand.

Nate takes initiative.

"What do you want? I bet you're a margarita girl, huh?"

The bartender makes eye contact with me, and I quickly look away. I stall.

"Hmm. I'm not sure, yet. You go ahead." Nate picks up the bar menu and asks the bartender for a few minutes to decide. The bartender, a short, Italian-looking guy with wet, slicked black hair tosses two square napkins our way and designates our spot for drinks.

My shaking intensifies, and the hand that Nate's not holding, I clinch to a fist. Will he serve me? Are the two napkins code for "go ahead and order, I'm not asking for your ID"?

Nate releases my hand to study the menu.

I'm a nervous wreck. I glance over at the bartender serving someone down the bar. He's yet to smile, and I can't get a read on this guy.

"I need to use the restroom. I'll just take whatever you get." I stretch myself taller to look over heads for the restroom.

"You sure?"

"Yeah, I'm sure. I'm easy."

He laughs and widens his eyes.

It dawns on me.

"I'm easy. Like easy to please . . . not easy like easy!"

He continues to laugh.

"Oh, you know what I mean!" I walk away to find the restroom.

I don't need to use it, so I check myself in the full length mirror for a few minutes and try to imagine what's going on between Nate and the bartender. When I walk out, Nate's right there.

"Hey, do you have your ID on you? He won't serve me two drinks without it . . . so ridiculous for a place like this."

I stammer, "Oh, yeah. Just a minute. I think I left my lipstick in there." I point back to the bathroom door and walk in. I'm frazzled. I look for an escape route. A tunnel. A loose ceiling tile that I can crawl through and hide. A secret passage that will lead me to the alley. I squat down and bow my head because I'm on the verge of fainting.

After a few minutes, I stand and walk back to the door and poke my head out.

"Hey, you go ahead. I'm not feeling real well. I'll catch

up in a sec."

"Are you okay? You don't look so well."

"Yeah, I'm fine. I just need a couple of minutes."

I close the door and regain my composure. Great. Just great. He probably thinks I'm in here with an upset stomach. How freaking embarrassing. The need to escape becomes greater.

I take deep breaths. Reapply my lipstick that doesn't need reapplied, and walk back out.

Nate's sitting at the bar now, drinking a beer. I make my way over and place my hand on his back. He turns and says, "Everything okay?"

"Yeah, everything's fine. Sorry, I just think my blood sugar was a little off."

"You're diabetic?"

"Oh, no . . . I just haven't eaten much today. That's all.'

"Want a drink?"

"Thanks, but I better not until I get something to eat."

Nate turns around and takes a swig from his beer. I notice the words on the label are not written in English. I keep my hand on his back. He's extra cute tonight. A pale blue, collared, cotton shirt. Starched khaki pants. We stand, unable to make a lot of conversation because of the crowd. Nate doesn't even finish his beer before they call us to our table, so he brings it with him.

It's slightly awkward since the tables are round. But the hostess helps us out by pulling out the chairs and assigning us a place to sit. We sit down directly across from each other.

He says, "You look great tonight, by the way. Your hair is extra beautiful."

I fight back a smile.

"Well, thank you."

I open my menu.

"So, what's good here?"

"Everything's good here. You really can't go wrong."

I decide on something safe and easy to eat: lasagna.

Without ever opening it, Nate pushes his menu to the side. He looks right into my eyes. "So, Chandra. Tell me about yourself."

I have a quick panic attack from the way he says my name. Does he know it's a cover? Did he just say that in an intentional I-know-everything-about-you tone? I pause, and then calmly respond. "Me? What do you want to know?"

He doesn't look away.

"Where are you from? Where do you work? Do you have family?"

I'm caught off guard.

"Um. Why?"

He laughs.

"Um. Because we're on a date, and I'm interested in getting to know you . . .?" A reply in question form.

I continue to look at my menu, although I know what I want.

"I was born in Newcastle, Oklahoma. I work at a tag office (*tag office*??!!!). I have a dad."

He sympathetically raises his eyebrows.

"That's it? Just a dad?"

"Well, I have other family members too, it's just my dad is the only one that I'm close to."

He looks like he wants to ask more questions but doesn't.

"Oh."

relief fills my lungs. "So. . . did you go to college?"

"Yep, OU. Boomer Sooner. I was a business major but got sidetracked with making money."

"You can always go back someday."

"Yeah, that might be difficult with a wife and three kids. Papa's gotta keep the lights on and the water running, ya know."

"Whatever." I push my leg against his under the table.

We flirt our way through dinner.

Chapter 23

When Nate suggests going to play poker after dinner, I slightly panic.

"You play poker?" I ask as we walk out onto the street.

"Yep. All casino workers play. Every one of them. We're basically slaves to the casino. Shoot, half those people never even make it home with a check."

This surprises me.

"Wow."

He's persistent on going to play poker, not in a casino, but at his friend's house. His buddies have been playing since they were fifteen . . . they're good guys . . . He'll make them watch their language.

I basically answer his question when I follow him to his car. Yes, of course I'll go.

He has a nice car for a guy in his early twenties. A black SUV, tinted windows, leather seats. The car chirps when Nate pushes his remote, and he walks to the passenger side to let me in. Being the non-drinker I am, I have a buzz going after the two margaritas at dinner. I grab the car door to steady myself, and hop into the best smelling vehicle I've ever stepped foot in. Did he spray men's cologne on the seats to make them smell this good?

He gets in, and we're off. The dashboard lights his face in the darkness, and he turns down his music to a perfect volume, one where we can listen and talk at the same time. Rolling Stones, "Beast of Burden." This makes him that much more attractive . . . Let's go home and draw the curtains.

We don't say much on the quick drive. His friend lives in a new downtown development—high-end apartments surrounded by a quaint sandwich shop and a cupcake bakery. Parking is difficult, and we drive around for at least ten minutes waiting for someone else to surrender their space. The margaritas are my saving grace; they've downgraded my shakes from convulsive to internal. I'm shaking on the inside, but I don't think it will be noticeable.

We walk up a brick pathway to a door with hanging plants. It's unusual that a bachelor would go through the trouble of hanging plants, but whatever. Noise behind the door lets us know that we've definitely found the party.

After three rings and no answer, Nate grabs my hand when we just walk in.

I hear voices, but I can't make out faces; the cigar smoke makes it difficult to see. We break through the cloud of smoke and, in unison, his buddies holler out, "Heeeey! It's Nate!"

"And a girl?!" A guy in a visor with a cigarette behind his ear lets me know I've just walked into a boys' club.

Nate waves his hand through the smoke. "This girl can outplay every single one of you amateurs. Give her some chips." Nate throws down $100 on a green felt table. It's a table straight out of a casino. In the formal dining area.

A scruffy looking guy in a hoodie takes a long hit off his cigar and demands, "Get the girl some chips." He slurs his words. "And a shot of Jack if she's going to run with this wolf pack." They consider it a good enough reason for a cheers! Glasses clink together, and they crack up so long it's forgotten what they were laughing about to begin with.

Drunk guys playing poker.

Really, really drunk guys playing poker.

Opportunity knocks.

Nate tells me he doesn't want to play against me. He pushes a fold up chair to the table, the kind you take with you on a camping trip. A guy in dark shades starts stacking my chips in front of me, and I sit down in the chair. It's embarrassing because my chair is shorter than everyone else's, and I'm sunk down about six inches lower than the other players. I can't stomach the Jack Daniels. There's no way. I hand mine to Nate, and he shoots it back and announces that will be his last. I hope so. He *is* driving!

Once I settle into my chair I start to look around the apartment. It's tidy. It's decorated in a cute, eclectic way . . . turquoise painted furniture, candles, and fresh flowers in milk glass vases . . . the exact opposite of a bachelor's pad. My eyes widen when I see the guy in the visor pictured on his wedding day. The classic picture: he's scooped her up in her gorgeous gown, and she's beautiful. He's married?! Oh my! Married?! I'm reminded of my youngness.

"Ante up, losers." The dealer calls the game. "Follow the queen."

"Yeah, he's always wanting to follow a queen." A player adds, and they all explode into laughter. Again.

I just smile politely, and Nate says, "Don't start it you guys, we have a lady in the house."

The same guy adds, "Lady in da house." In his best high-pitched, hip-hop voice.

I pull closer to the table, and take a look at my cards. I'm two margaritas brave. I clear my voice and say, "May the best man win."

The cards are good to me, and my stack grows quickly.

About an hour into it, the guy's wife comes home. She goes toward the living area and pulls a blanket from an old trunk that's being used as a coffee table. She sits down, turns on the television, and makes herself comfy. I think about how cool it is to be married and all grown up. She flips through the channels, and rests her head on a throw pillow tolerating the rowdy group of boys acting like they're at a frat house.

Nate hollers over to her.

"Amber, come here. I want you to meet someone."

We make eye contact; she smiles, then gets up and walks to the table.

"This is Chandra." Nate nods his head to me.

She offers her hand. "Hi, I'm Amber." She looks me up and down to the point of extreme discomfort.

She knows.

She knows I'm young.

Girls have that instinct.

She knows I'm young and don't belong here.

"It's nice to meet you, Amber." I say, then turn back to Nate and whisper that we better get going.

Nate's ready too.

"Cash the lady out."

Everyone rebukes.

"What? You guys are leaving?" They're all in a tizzy.

"You heard me. Cash the lady out. It's my bedtime."

The word "bedtime" is received as one last hilarious revelation.

One guy elbows his neighbor and says, "Oh, it's his bedtime, alright." And they laugh and strengthen the ties that bind the boys' club to which they belong.

Nate does laugh, but plays it off with, "We've gotta get out of here before things get really ugly. Amber, they're all yours, honey."

Amber's not amused. You can tell this isn't her first time to deal with cigar smoke and sloppy drunks.

"Gee, thanks. I'm so lucky."

Her husband likes this comment.

"Luckier than a leprechaun with a winning lottery ticket." And the crowd goes wild.

I'm smiling but more focused on the money that's being counted out: $257.

I needed this. I really, really needed this.

Amber walks us to the door and politely says the, "It was nice to meet you," line. I wonder how many "nice to meet yous" Amber has dealt with over the years.

We walk out the door, and I hand Nate back the $100 I started with. He grabs my hand and pulls me close to him. "We should get you on the poker circuit; you're a money-makin' machine."

"Yeah, it doesn't always go that way."

He drives me to my parking lot, pulls behind my car, and shifts to park. "I had a great time tonight, Chandra."

I'm melting.

"Me too. I had a great time."

"I'll follow you home to make sure you get in safely."

"No." I stumble with my words. "I mean, thanks, but I'll be fine."

He squints at me like I'm hiding something, and I know he knows there's a piece of the puzzle missing. I just pray he doesn't find it.

Chapter 24

I sit in the back of math class Monday morning and do some real-life math figuring on a scratch sheet of paper. My teacher's talking ratios when I realize that even with my weekend win we are still short on rent and bill money. Way short. Not to mention I still owe Cass $100 bucks. I'm a million miles away, and people and teachers around me are the equivalent of static radio background noise. There's a test I didn't study for waiting on my desk when I get to Spanish. I look around and everyone else is cranking out answers. I look back and stare at the paper, but I really don't care. I'd rather be at the casino. I think about Nate and playing poker.

I avoid Cassidy, again, and make it through the day and after-school practice without talking to her. I get the feeling Cassidy's beginning to distance herself from me too, and right now I'm okay with that.

I want everything about high school and cheer to go away.

A second date with Nate is just what the doctor ordered. He tells me it's a surprise and to dress comfortably. I put on a loose fitting cotton dress (a two dollar bargain from the Goodwill), look in the mirror, and decide it's perfect. Periwinkle-colored cotton and it's the perfect length to show off my thighs. I pull my hair back in a messy bun, and I try hard to look cute in a "comfortable" kind of way. I do, however, deviate from comfortable and put on my new boots because they are just that fabulous.

We meet at a gas station, because I tell him my house is too hard to find and it will make things easier. I go weak in the knees when I pull in and see him waiting for me in his SUV.

I strap my purse across my chest and bend down where he can't see me so I can squirt some body spray on my neck. Mango and watermelon. He walks to me first. Opens my door, and reaches in to give me a kiss on the cheek. Thank God I thought to remove my algebra book from the passenger seat.

"Wow." Nate looks me up and down when I step out of the car. "You look great." He reaches in for another kiss on the cheek. "You smell great too. Maybe we should just forget what I have planned and . . ." He laughs. He's testing the waters, and I'm already in the pool.

"So where *are* we going on this mystery date?" I grab his hand and we walk toward his Tahoe.

Just like last time, it's this overwhelming feeling of excitement when he opens the door for me and I step into his leathery man cave of a car. He walks around to his side, gets in, and starts the car, and I'm ready to go *anywhere* with this boy. Guy. Man-boy . . . or whatever he is.

"Well, it's a surprise. You'll see when we get there." He starts the car then pulls out into the traffic. The music adds to the mood, set at a perfect volume where we can still talk about things like bands, sushi (I do my best), and some of the regular characters in the poker room.

He makes his way to the highway and merges on in the most masculine way possible. I fantasize that we're leaving town. And will be gone for a very, very long time.

"So I want to know more." Nate reaches for the radio volume knob, and turns the music down just a tad.

"More?" I ask.

"Yeah. More . . . about you. Like your job. Where you live. Your hobbies. Your family . . . You know, more about you."

I pause.

Hobbies. I can do hobbies.

"Well, I don't really have time for many hobbies. I watch cooking shows sometimes. I like to cook."

"A hot chick who likes to cook? Must be my lucky day."

I leave out the part that I could lie on the couch and watch Bobby Flay smoke salmon all day, but a grilled cheese and bowl of cereal are basically the only things on my menu.

He's intrigued.

"What's your favorite thing to cook?"

"Hmmm." Think.

Think.

Think.

"My favorite thing to cook . . . Hmmm . . ." I try to think of something impressive that I can pronounce correctly, and the inside of our refrigerator makes an appearance in my head. Milk. Cheese. Juice and butter. "I like to cook fish a lot. Salmon, tuna, trout." (Tuna, as in canned, but we'll leave out that little detail as well.)

"Impressive." He says, then moves onto the next subject. "So what do you do at the tag office?"

Tag office? What is he talking about?

I scrunch my eyebrows and continue looking forward.

"Didn't you say you worked at a tag agency or something?"

I'm going to have to start writing this stuff down.

"Oh, yeah. I thought you said *rag* office, and I was like, what?" I reach for a piece of gum in my purse. "I just do tag stuff. You know, car tags and boat tags and stuff like that. Pretty boring, actually."

I make a mental note that I grill tuna steaks and hate my pretend full-time job.

"So where are we going?"

Off the highway there's a beautiful sunset on a small lake with sailboats. Never in my life did I know that a single sailboat existed in Oklahoma. "Are we on Northside?" I ask.

He laughs, "Yep, we've been traveling north. You know, Lake Hefner. Haven't you been here before?"

Um, no.

"Well, *yes*." Of course, all twenty-somethings have been to Lake Hefner, and that would include me.

Nate pulls off the highway and crosses an overpass to navigate his way into a parking lot. There are a few restaurants, *nice* restaurants, and the parking lot is full. I feel like we're out of town in a faraway place, but it was only a twenty-minute car ride. There's an outdoor band setting up on a big lawn area, and I can't believe this place is twenty minutes from where I live.

"I love it out here," I say, "it's so beautiful." We get out of the car and I wonder if we're headed toward the gourmet Mexican food restaurant or the steakhouse.

Nate grabs my hand, and we walk in silence through the parking lot. Then, he starts walking toward the boat dock, and I think we're going to go sit on the park bench for a little while before dinner. How romantic.

When we get to the end of the boat dock he looks down at my boots.

"Those are cool boots. And you're smokin' hot in them and all, but you'll probably want to slip them off."

Two thoughts on this:

1. He thinks I'm smokin' hot in my boots.

2. Why am I taking them off?

He waits, and I just give him a blank stare . . .

Water sloshes up on the sailboat we're standing next to, and he nods toward it.

"What?" I ask.

"Take your boots off, and let's go."

"Oh my gosh. This is yours?"

He smiles and nods toward my boots. "Yes, it's all mine. Now let's go."

Is this a dream? I'm standing here in designer boots about to board a sailboat with a twenty-two-year-old pit boss. Basically the complete opposite of my real life. I wait for a purple dragon to drop from the sky to confirm this is definitely a dream as I start to take off my boots.

It's embarrassing because as cute as my boots are, they

are an absolute pain to get off. It usually takes me at least five minutes to get them off. There's no way to make this graceful or attractive. I sit on my butt, and Nate reaches down to help.

We begin the struggle.

"This is so embarrassing."

"Don't be embarrassed. Personally, I kinda like it," Nate laughs as he acts like he's looking up my dress.

I pull on my dress to make sure I stay covered as we wrangle around. It's a full-fledged tug-o-war before both boots come off. I'm glad we're outside in the open air so hopefully the stinky boot-sock smell doesn't reach his nose. He helps me onto the boat, and off we go.

It's straight out of a Jennifer Aniston romcom. Nate pushes off the dock, rolls up the sleeves on his shirt, then grabs the oars. The sun is setting, the water makes perfect lapping noises against the boat, and Nate's muscles flex every time he rows. For a good while, we don't even speak. He just rows away from the noise of live music and couples eating on patios. I look around at the beautiful scenery and get a better understanding of what it means when people use the word "surreal."

He stops rowing for just a moment so he can point at two ducks. "Ha! Look. They're on a date too."

"They are! How cute," I laugh. The fact that Nate observes two ducks on a date makes me melt.

"I wonder if he's nervous."

I cock my head and watch them for a while.

"No, he's not. She's a nervous wreck, though. Look at her." We watch the ducks swimming around. I love that this conversation is so senseless. I love that for the first time, in a really long time, there's a part of my life that seems easy.

"I bet she needed a night on the town, what with the eight kids and all," he adds.

"Nope. I bet it's their first date. He's wondering about first base."

Nate cocks a smile at me then looks away. He rows toward the center of the lake until the noise becomes faint. A breeze begins to blow my hair around, and Nate lets go of an oar and brushes a strand behind my ear. He rubs his hand over his own shaved head.

"Sorry, my hair's getting all messed up."

I laugh. I laugh at everything he says. I couldn't dream up a more romantic, fun date if I tried. It's perfect. Everything about Nate is perfect, and when it all comes to an end for the night, we make it to first base. Okay. Second. Rounding second.

That night, before I fall asleep, I decide two things:

1. It would be really easy to fall in love with Nate.
2. I don't have time for cheer.

Chapter 25

On Monday I drive to school thirty minutes earlier than usual. There's a low fog, and everything seems wet. I'm sure the teachers are already at school, standing around swapping stories and waking up with their coffee, preparing for a whole new day in the glory of educating teenagers.

Miss Mound isn't in her room when I get there, so I sit down in a chair and try to look miserable. I sit in silence for a few minutes until she walks in.

"Oh no! What happened?!" She places her bags and coffee on a student desk in the back.

I force my eyes to get teary.

"I was carrying a box to my car and lost my footing stepping off the porch. I'm so sorry." I pick my crutches up off the floor to make sure she sees them. "The doctor said it's not broken, but I have to stay in this boot for six to eight weeks."

"Six to eight weeks?" She comes around to get a closer look.

"Yeah."

"Well, hmm. Nothing you can do about that." She puts her hands on her hips and stares at the boot.

A tear drops down my cheek.

Cassidy sees me hobbling to my first class, and I tell her before she has a chance to ask.

"Tripped off the porch."

Her eyebrows scrunch.

"Sheesh. Are you kidding me?!"

"I was carrying a box and misjudged where the step was."

She looks like she's stepped out of a magazine. Dressy high-heel boots, leggings, and a cute chunky sweater. She swings a new, giant Michael Kors bag onto her shoulder.

"Do you need help?"

"Nah, I got it." My canvas bag hangs from my wrist so my hands are able to wrap around the crutches' handles. "Oh, I'll have your money soon. Probably the first of next week, if that's okay."

She stares at me without words. She knows me too well, and this isn't a good thing at the time.

"Chelsea, keep the money. I don't care about that. I'm just worried about you. You've been so non-existent; you've completely separated yourself from everything and everyone. And now this?" She points to my boot.

"I'm fine. Really, I'm fine."

"What'd Miss Mound say?"

"I told her with the injury that there's not much I can do. She said that's fine, just bring her a doctor's note."

"How are you going to do that?"

"What do you mean how am I going to do that?"

'The doctor's note?"

"I'm going to bring her a doctor's note." I say firmly.

"So you're really hurt?"

I roll my eyes and walk away.

After school I pull to the back of a dry cleaner's parking lot and shift my car to park. I keep the engine running as I remove the boot and grab my crutches. I get out—thanking God that that's over for the day—and pop the trunk. I'd always thought crutches were so cool when I was little, but now my opinion is quite different after a day of underarm pain.

When I drive home, Dad's sitting on the porch waiting for me.

He never does this.

Chapter 26

He doesn't take his eyes off me as I park and walk to the door.

Shit. He knows. He knows something.

Nate.

The gambling.

Electric bill cut-off notice.

He clasps his hands, brings them under his chin, and says nothing.

Shit. What is it?

It's the D in Spanish.

Quitting the squad.

It's the injury. He knows I've faked an injury.

The date?

Me drinking?

I smile the "I'm-confused" smile and say, "Hello?"

"Hi honey."

Something is so off.

"Dad, what's wrong?"

He doesn't move. He just sits for a while.

It's the gambling. He knows.

It has to be the gambling.

He takes a deep breath and extends his legs.

"Honey." He pauses. I'm busted. It's a for sure, definite bust. He crosses his legs at the ankles and leans back onto his elbows. "I don't want you to worry, but I quit my job last night. Things may start to get a little tight."

I'm relieved, mad, and shocked all at once.

"Dad? You quit your job? What!"

He can't look at me.

"I just can't do it anymore. It's the same ol' thing day-in and day-out, and I'm just ready for a change. Things will look up and get better for us eventually, I promise. But I was thinking if I sell your car and some things around the house it will get us through a month or two, and by then I'll have an even better job making more money. You can use my pick-up to get to school, and I'll job hunt in the evenings and on the weekends." Tears fill my eyes so I turn away where he can't see me.

"We'll be okay, Dad. We'll make it work somehow," I say as I walk through the door.

Chapter 27

I start with fifty-two dollars. I'm limited on time—with Dad not working and all—he'll be home to check up on me. So, I go straight after school. Dad thinks I'm at practice. Technically I'm not lying about it, it's just that I haven't got around to telling him that I quit.

Nate's off on Wednesdays, and I'm glad about that because I need to stay focused. I'm standing at the check-in counter for less than ten minutes when he sends me a text (first one ever!) that says, "Hi. You're playin' tonight?"

I read it, then start to look around. Where is he? How does he know this?

I text back. "Are you here?"

He responds, "No."

I keep looking around.

"Um, then how do you know I'm here?"

After a slight delay, he responds, "I have eyes all over that casino."

I look up at the cameras in the ceiling. I look around

at the other employees. Who is watching me? And what's more, who has Nate told about me? I start to bite the skin around my thumbnail.

I'm standing right there in front of the guy who pulls the microphone over and says, "Chandra, your no limit table is ready . . . Chan-dra, come on down." He gets immense pleasure out of pretending he's on *The Price is Right*. I raise my pointer finger to signal that, Hel-lo guy, I'm Chandra. Remember me from just ten minutes ago?

"Table six, Chandra." He makes that clicking sound to go along with his wink. "Good luck."

I breathe in. I breathe out. Once again, it's good to be home.

When I sit down and place my three twenties on the table I request single dollar chips. I hate it when they chip me in fives because the stack seems so small. There are two regulars at the table, and they all smile and acknowledge me entering the game. The dealer, a familiar face too, reaches for my twenties. I keep my phone in my lap. She tucks my twenties into her tray then readjusts a bobby pin holding her blond, short hair behind her ear.

It's my third hand that doubles my stack.

But I need more.

I stare back at the screen displaying table games, and I become curious about what it takes to play on a higher-stakes table. After a few smaller wins, I get up the nerve to ask the dealer. I'm glad to be sitting right next to her, and I keep my voice low.

"So how much do you need to start with to play on the 5-10 table?"

She leans toward me as she continues to deal the cards, multitasking being a prerequisite to poker dealing.

"Eh, the pots can get pretty big over there. It just depends what kind of player you are. The key is to double-up fast because you just have more power with a big stack."

I shake my head and look at the cards I've been dealt. "Could you start with a couple hundred dollars?" She turns over the community cards.

"Mmm, yeah. But I wouldn't start with any less than that."

I'm holding a pair with a pair on the board; the bet makes its way to me.

"I'm all in." I push $120—give or take—to the middle.

People toss in their cards without even waiting their turn. All but one, a young kid with curly hair and ear buds. He's staring at his hold cards, tapping them up and down, and bobbing his head to whatever music it is he's listening to. He knows it's his move, but he can't get a read on me. I start playing with my phone in my lap.

The dealer, in a whisper, says, "No phones during a hand," so I quickly stick it in my purse. She taps her fingers on his side of the table and says, "We need a call or a fold," and he pulls out one ear bud. She repeats, "We need a call or a fold." He starts to count out his chips, and the dealer confirms its $118 for the call. He counts them out, separates them from his stack, but chooses to sit there a bit longer to ponder his hand.

Players get antsy. One speaks up.

"Come on already."

He's not intimidated by the player's comment, and at this point I begin to worry about his hand. There's no way he'd be agonizing if it was all that good. No way.

He cocks his head like why-the-hell-am-I-doing-this

and pushes the pre-counted stack toward the middle.

I toss my cards down—two pair—and I hear a regular say, "She went all in with that?!"

My opponent looks at my cards, really studies them, and chooses not to reveal his own. He puts his ear bud back in and leans on the table to rest his chin in the palm of his hand.

"Good hand," my neighbor says. Then the players chatter and there's nine kinds of speculation and assessment over what it was he had and why he stayed.

I get up to get a tray.

And get my name back on the list.

Chapter 28

I'm standing by a slot machine waiting for my table when I come close to having a heart attack.

"Boo," he says and scares me. I jump, turn toward him, and my instant reaction is to cover my chip tray with my hand.

He laughs.

"I'm not stealing your chips, Beautiful." It's Nate. He's in blue jeans and a ball cap. The cutest ball cap I've ever seen in my whole life. Okay. The cutest guy wearing a ball cap that I've ever seen in my whole life.

"What are you doing here?" It's obvious he's not working since he's in street clothes.

"Oh, just out and about. Thought it'd be a perfect time to pick up my check since I heard my favorite player was here. Are you waiting for a table?"

"Yeah, I'm just switching tables."

"Switching?" He nods toward my chips. "It looks like you're doing pretty good to me."

"Oh, I'm not switching to shake off some bad mojo.

I'm going to try a 5-10 table."

"Ooooo. A 5-10 table, huh? She's big-time now." He speaks of me in third person.

I decide to do the same.

"Do you think she's stupid?"

Nate puts his hand on my back and kisses my cheek.

"I think she can play anything she wants to."

I look up at the cameras behind tinted glass in the ceilings and I can't believe he just did that. He kissed me at his work. Who saw that? He kissed me at his work! I tingle, to say the least, like jumping in a cold swimming pool.

"Chandra, your 5-10 no limit seat is ready. Chaaaaaaaandra." The announcer gets his mouth way too close to the microphone.

Nate pats my back. "You're up."

"Are you going to be around here?" I ask hoping the answer is no.

"Yeah, I'll be around. Good luck." He walks with no particular direction.

My assigned table is front and center, so I take just a few steps and sit down in the empty seat. I don't know what to expect and not one single player looks familiar. My eyes get big when I see the mound of chips in the center, and there are very few white chips that make up the heap.

Good Mother of All Big Pots. Is this normal?

I don't want to give away that I'm a high-stakes virgin, so I don't say a word and watch the hand pan out. A man with silver hair calls a bet by tossing even more colored chips to the center, and no words are spoken. The dealer even remains silent. It's understood who does what and when it's done. The dealer looks so sleepy, and it's totally by default, because he's got droopy sacks under his bloodshot eyes. He's seemingly too tired to speak until the very end of the hand when he says, "Let's see 'em."

The opposing players turn over the cards and little emotion is shown by either of them.

The guy with silver hair doesn't care that he lost.

And the twenty-something guy shows no excitement in winning around $800 (and that's just me counting the chips I could see). It takes one hand for me to realize that it's a whole different card game over here. After witnessing this, I feel like I've been playing Chutes and Ladders the past month.

It's totally embarrassing when I get my chips. These big dogs have no less than $1000 each in front of them, and one guy on the table could purchase a used car with what he's sitting with.

Still, no words.

It's so uncomfortable I have the urge to strike up a conversation just for the sake of changing the mood. I clear my voice.

"So, you think it's going to rain tonight?" I say to no one in particular.

No one answers, but maybe they just didn't hear me. I take a peek at my cards and almost hate that I'm dealt such good cards so early in my game. I would rather sit here awhile and get a feel for the table, but there's no way you can toss your cards back in when you're holding two kings.

You just can't.

The betting moves around the table, and when it gets to me I must pay thirty dollars to keep the royalty in my hands (it's just the first round of betting). I'm out of my league. Do people really play at this level? What do these people do for a living? Doctors? Lawyers? CEOs? One thing's for sure, they're not high school kids ordering off the dollar menu at McDonald's.

I call.

I stop breathing as the dealer flops over the community cards. Two. Ace. Ace.

Not good. I punish myself by thinking of all the things I could have spent that thirty bucks on. A sack of groceries. A flat iron. A half a tank of gas.

I notice the players getting fidgety . . . one lights a cigarette, one leans back in his chair, and one takes off his glasses and rubs them down with a handkerchief.

They can't have the ace.

Another round of betting, another thirty dollars, and I decide there's no turning back now.

A guy with a clean-shaven face—the shiny with moisturizer kind—forces me to go all-in.

I have to. I'm already too invested in this pot. I can't stand the thought of folding now, with all my chips that sit in the middle.

It's pocket change to him.

It's everything to me.

Do. Not. Have. The. Ace. I eat at my cuticle. I sit on my foot to get a better view.

I don't have time to think about the $200 plus I have in the middle.

Because I can't even tell you what the guy had, what the last card was, or what the dealer said.

It's all a blur.

I fade out. It's like swimming underwater with a leaky

mask.

I come to when the guy next to me nudges my arm and says, "It's your pot, little lady. Pull it in."

I look at him. In slow motion.

I look at the pot. In slow motion.

My arms are heavy, but I manage to stand and start scooping the chips to form stacks. Chip colors I ain't EVER seen before.

I sit through three hands without betting. I've heard people talk about a runner's high before. I'm curious to know what chemicals my brain is currently releasing to create this gambler's high of mine. I feel like laughing, crying, and screaming. It's that feeling when your foot falls asleep, except this is a whole-body experience.

Against Kenny Rogers' better judgment, I start counting my money at the table. I can't help myself. I separate the colors, and come to a grand total of $722.

That's almost a $500 gain, in JUST ONE HAND.

I can't believe it. This definitely puts a Band Aid on things. For now.

It's so easy, this high-stakes table.

It's so incredibly easy.

I look on the dealer's ID badge, to find his name. "Jim, can I please get a tray? I think I'm done here."

Nate meets me at the cashier. "Well, well. If it ain't Ms. Annie Duke herself."

I have no idea what he's talking about. He sees I have no idea what he's talking about. "You know, Annie Duke. The Duke. Annie Legend. The Duchess of Poker."

Still, no idea what he's talking about, but I fake it with a giggle. "Oh yeah, Annie."

I like that Nate's here next to me. I like that he knew

when I finished, and he's already here. He whispers in my ear, "You need help getting that out to your car, ma'am?" He steps back and winks at me.

He kisses me, again on the cheek, when he tucks me safely into my car and sends me on my way. He'll call me tomorrow. Maybe we can do lunch. Lunch? That would be next to impossible considering high school kids get forty-five minutes for lunch. I envision Nate picking me up in the circle drive in front of my high school, me bouncing out with a backpack. *Um, no.*

Although my winnings are already earmarked, I decide to indulge in yet one small treat. I've always heard about people getting pedicures, seen the little designs of flowers, pumpkins, or whatever the occasion called for. For a split second my throat tightens when I think about it because this is such a mother-daughter activity. Cassidy and her mom go every other Thursday and call it "Date Night." But I shake it off, because today it's my turn.

Stella. I'll swing by Miss Stella's and ask if she'd like to join. I pull her card from my wallet to check the address then drive thirty minutes to her side of town.

Her poofy white dog starts barking like crazy when I ring the doorbell. I can see him through the screen door balancing on his hind legs, yelping to his master that a visitor is on their porch.

Stella scoops up the yippy thing and opens the door to greet me. She's in a turquoise jogging suit, showing off her petite, little figure, and it's weird to see her in something so casual.

"Hi," *bark, bark-bark, bark,* "Miss Stella."

"Well hello, Chandra. What a nice surprise." The dog calms after Stella approves of me.

"Stella, I came by to see if you wanted to splurge with me. I'm going to get a pedicure. Wanna come?"

Stella kicks off her fancy flip-flop and examines her toes for a few seconds. Pretty feet for an old lady, not the jumbled up toes one would expect. "A pedicure, huh?"

"Yeah, a pedi, like they say. Let's go get a pedi, Miss Stella."

She giggles and says, "Something I've never done in my life!"

"Well that makes two of us. Let's do it!"

I remember seeing a little place tucked in the corner of a strip mall, sandwiched nicely between a copy shop and a sushi take-out, so that's where I take us. We walk in, and there's a strong scent of fingernail polish and chemicals. Three clipboards with sign-in sheets sit on the counter, and there are workers everywhere, but they're too busy to greet us. I grab the 'pedicure' clipboard and write STELLA, then write my name underneath.

Miss Stella smiles at me and glances at the clipboard. Her eyebrows scrunch in shock, like there's something she doesn't understand.

"Chelsea? Who's Chelsea?"

My eyes widen. I can't believe I've made such a stupid mistake. I start formulating lies at a very rapid pace. Chelsea's my middle name . . . Chandra's a nickname . . . my head spins with ideas, but I just can't do it. I can't lie to Miss Stella.

After a few seconds, she breaks the silence.

"Chelsea, huh." She grabs my hand and squeezes. "Chelsea. Well I think that's a beautiful name."

She asks no questions.

This makes me emotional, and I fight back tears as

a worker dressed in a white smock leads us back to our chairs.

The worker starts filling the foot baths with water and tosses in some blue crystal-looking rocks. I'm not sure what to do, and Stella and I stand and wait for directions. The worker, in tall heels revealing longish red toenails with rhinestones, points to the chairs and it's our signal to sit down.

Stella giggles when she's out of her comfort zone. I've noticed this about her at the poker table. So she can't stop giggling when she pulls her jogging pants to her knees, sits down, and sticks her feet in the blue bubbly water.

"Oooooweeeeee. Boy, this is the life!" she says, then closes her eyes and leans her head back in relaxation. I take a minute to stare. She's a beautiful woman, Miss Stella.

Another worker walks up and hands me a remote, but I'm confused because there's no television in sight.

"Massage." The worker says, and I realize that I'm sitting in a massage chair like I've seen at the mall. Neck. Upper back. Lower back. I get to choose. I press the button for lower back, and I'm feeling like a queen.

I worry that Stella thinks I'm a fraud. She has to know something's not right with me, that Chandra is some kind of fake. I wonder if she knows it's my age that I'm hiding. Still, no questions, and I already know she won't pry. That's not her style.

I dip my feet into the water and mimic Stella by leaning my head back and closing my eyes. The jets feel fabulous. I can't believe people get to do this all the time. A real treat!

The worker asks, "Where's your color?" and this

is when I realize that we were supposed to pick out our polish before we sat down. Oops.

"I'll just take that teal color on the end," I say.

Stella says, "Me too."

We smile at each other, Stella and me, but we don't speak another word. We don't have to.

After an hour of sheer foot bliss—salt scrubs, massages and lotion—the petite lady paints my toes. It's the best my feet have ever looked. Ever. I tilt my head and stare down at my toes.

"Dad, how do you get toe paint?" It was a hot summer day. I was barefoot. We sat on the porch steps.

"Toe paint?"

"Yeah, toe paint."

"Like paint for the walls?"

"No, toe paint."

"Honey, I'm not sure what you mean. Are you talking about paint?"

I wiped the sweat off my forehead, then showed him with my index finger.

"No, Dad. Like this." My pointer finger started painting my big toenail.

He got it.

"Ooohhh. Toe paint. You're talking about fingernail polish." He laughed.

"No, Dad. FOR YOUR TOES, NOT YOUR FINGERS."

He laughed some more.

"Well, you're right. It's nail polish. They call it nail polish, I

think."

"Can we get some? The girls at my school have red and pink." I continued painting with my finger.

"Well, sure honey, we'll find you some polish for these pretty little toes." He reached over and started tickling them. "We can paint them like this, and like this . . . oh, and how about like this . . ." He tickled in between my toes.

I was laughing so hard I could hardly get the words out, ". . . Stop, Daddy!"

That night Dad painted my toes. Pink.

Miss Stella loves hers too. It makes me laugh when she says, "Oh yes!" when asked if she wants a design. "I'll take some daisies. Yes, daisies for sure!" She talks me into it too, and we leave with the prettiest daisy feet you've ever seen in your life.

We become buddies, Miss Stella and me, and it helps to get my mind off of going to the casino. I drive to her place for dinner a couple of nights, and she spoils me rotten with home-cooked meals and yummy desserts. I walk around her living room and look at framed pictures as she sets the table in the kitchen. I learn that she has three kids, all out of state. This isn't a comfortable subject for Miss Stella, so I don't ask questions, just look at the photos and try to figure out what happened to what seemed to be a perfectly happy family.

"Smells good, Miss Stella! What is it tonight?" I don't

know who enjoys this more, the giver or the receiver.

She pulls the lid from some smell-good on the stovetop and smoke rolls into the air. "Ziti and meatballs. Garlic bread and tea for my girl."

My girl. Miss Stella has started using this when she talks about me.

She asks for me to set the table, and I move to the kitchen to help her out.

It's as if we have this mutual unspoken understanding—you don't ask me about my life, and I won't ask about yours. And it works. She doesn't have to have a degree in psychology to figure out that I'm missing something in my life.

We sit at the table, and I chew extra slowly to savor the tastes of her food. Home-cooked meals have always been a fantasy on television until now. Miss Stella talks about things like flowers, recipes, and a gardening show she likes to watch. I listen, and tell her it would be neat to grow your own vegetables.

She wipes the corners of her mouth with her napkin and says, "Well, that's a project for us, then, Chandra. Next spring."

"What's that?" I ask.

"You and I. We'll build a garden in my backyard."

"Sounds fun. Let's do it!" I'm excited about the garden, but even more excited that this little rendezvous is going to last until spring! It's a feeling like a blanket being wrapped around me—a feeling of relief. A haven, a retreat.

After a bite of garlic bread, I close my eyes. "Mmm. This is so delicious, Miss Stella. I don't think I've ever had such good food in my life. Take that back. I KNOW I've never had such good, homemade food in my life."

"Well, you're welcome."

Chapter 29

Nate and I move to the next level, talking several times a day, keeping tabs on each other via text, yada, yada, yada. And it's after a few more dates that I'm sitting in the back in Spanish discretely writing checks for a couple of bills when I feel my phone vibrate. I check the number and see that it's Nate. I jump up and hobble to grab the restroom pass, and by the fifth ring I'm in the bathroom across the hall.

"Hello?" I say softly hoping no one can hear.

"Hey there." Nate says.

I smile and twist my hair with my finger and notice that I never twist my hair with my finger. "Hey. How's it goin'?"

"I'm good. What are you up to?"

"Oh, just working." I stare in the mirror and do more hair twisting.

"Well, I won't keep ya," Nate talks faster than usual, "I just had a crazy idea and wanted to throw it out there and see what you thought."

"Oh yeah, what's that?"

"I thought that we could go to Tulsa Saturday and stay at the casino there. I have some business to take care of, but I'd love your company. It's not too far of a drive. We could drive up tomorrow afternoon, stay the night, then come home Sunday. A little getaway."

My eyes go big in the mirror. Did he just say what I think he just said?!

"Tulsa?" A getaway sounds so grown-up.

"Yeah, it's a sister casino of ours, and they have a nice hotel attached. It's awesome."

Someone flushes in a stall, and I realize I'm not alone. I cup my phone with my hand hoping that Nate can't hear the echo of the flush and step into the corner to try to escape it.

"Yeah, that sounds like fun. I'm in!"

"Cool. I'll get 'er booked then," he says. "I'll let you get back to work."

I go back to class and all I can think about is a weekend with Nate. A WHOLE ENTIRE WEEKEND WITH NATE. Like overnight. This is what couples do. This is what people in love do. We'll have a grown-up dinner, and what will I wear? Will it be fancy or casual?

I walk out of Spanish in a cloud of blissful thoughts.

Nate and I make arrangements to meet at his place. I tell him my house is an embarrassing mess since I've been so busy at work, and it'll just be easier if I come to him. He buys it.

My hands are shaky, and I grip the steering

wheel as I look for his apartment. Directions that I've chicken-scratched on the back of an envelope sit on my console, and I feel like I'm in a dream.

He's given me the gate code to enter his complex, and this makes me feel even closer to him. Almost like a girlfriend with a key to the front door or something like that. I'm ecstatic, to say the least, and it feels like we're a couple or something when I pull my car into a numbered parking space right beside his. I grab my canvas bag with my overnight stuff, step out of the car, and readjust my clothing from the car ride. Perfect.

When Nate answers the door and smiles, I melt. It feels as if warm wax moves through my veins as I step inside. He kisses my cheek. Melt. Melt. Melt.

"Hi there, beautiful." More melting. More melting. More melting.

"Good to see you." I say as I receive the kiss.

I laugh to myself when I realize that less than twenty-four hours ago I was sitting in class learning to conjugate verbs and ask for directions in Spanish. Now I'm standing in Nate's apartment ready for a road trip. *Muy bueno.*

I look around his apartment. Nothing fancy, but there's a huge flat screen TV with a football game on. He's such a manly man. He takes one last look at the score before he turns it off, then grabs his duffle bag and says, "Let's do it."

I feel like a five-year-old when I set my canvas bag next to his luggage-like duffel in the backseat. A small piece of luggage gets added to my mental to buy list, and I kick myself for not buying that nice one at the Goodwill last time I was there. But who knew I'd have a need for a piece of luggage? Ha!

I think of Dad and my plan as Nate opens the passenger door for me. I slide in and tell myself DO NOT FORGET TO CALL DAD. Do. Not. Forget.

It's a perfect, and I do mean perfect, fall day. The sun is shining, there's no wind, and the leaves are at their beautiful peak. He plugs his phone into the console, and his music begins to play. The Beatles' "Something" sets the mood, and I'm already wishing this trip was going to be longer than a weekend.

I dodge some bullets on the way there by answering questions like: How was work this week? And give appropriate answers such as, "Oh, you know, work is work, I suppose."

There's a magnetic force in the car that makes me sit closer to the console than my door. I am over-the-top excited to be spending time with him. I like him more and more each minute. He makes me smile and laugh all the way to Tulsa.

You can see the casino from the interstate, and he points to show me.

"That's where we're going."

"Wow, that's cool." I say. Colorful lights flash, even in the daytime, and you can tell that the place is hoppin' by looking at the parking lot.

Nate takes the exit, and I try to contain my excitement. I pray since this is a "sister" casino that they won't be checking IDs at the door either. That would take this fairytale to a screeching halt in no time.

Nate pulls into valet parking, and he knows the guy that comes to park our car.

"Hey there, Brother Nate." They fist pump and slap

each other on the back.

"Hey Eddie, long time no see." Nate says.

Eddie opens the back door to help us with our bags. "You need some help getting this up to your room? Is this it?"

"Nah, we got it." Nate grabs my bag and hands it to me. I put the strap on my shoulder then I hide it behind my back so no one can see. Nate hands the guy some cash. The guy looks me up and down and gives Nate the nod and a wink.

We walk in through a grandiose entrance, and I immediately notice that this one smells much better than the one back home. Nate says, "Give me just a minute, and I'll get us checked in."

"Sure," I reply.

I stand in the elevated lobby and look down onto the casino floor. I see no one checking IDs, and there's no security or anyone official-looking at the entrance down by the stairs. I roll my shoulders back and take a couple of deep breaths.

You are eighteen.

There's a cool vibe in this place. Good music, lots of people, and it seems to be more of a social gathering compared to our casino.

"Here ya go." Nate walks up holding a little envelope. He opens it up and says, "Room 314."

"Oh, thanks." I take the plastic card. It takes me a minute to figure out the card is a room key.

"Did you remember to bring your Player's Club Card? Because it works here, too."

I stammer.

"Oh, no, I didn't even think about that." Because I

don't have one.

"No problem, we can go get you another one after we put our bags up." He starts walking to the elevators.

I panic.

I can't do that.

A Player's Club Card is for people of age with identification like a driver's license.

No.

No, no, no.

Nate punches our floor number in the elevator, and I start chewing my thumb.

He reaches to take my bag for me and I say, "That's okay, I got it."

When we get to the room, Nate slides his key in a slit, and a green light flashes for us to enter. I've never seen anything like this in my life. Wow. Just wow. We walk into the room and it's perfectly tidy. A cozy loveseat sits in the corner, along with a desk and a floor lamp. The comforter on the bed looks like it's been starched and pressed. There's a welcome basket on the desk wrapped in cellophane and topped with a shimmery bow. The small card reads "Nate and Chandra." My eyes widen when I see my name. Well, fake name.

"Wow, this is really nice." I say.

Nate says that his Tulsalites treat him good.

I'm dying to open up the gift basket, but Nate acts like it's no big thing, so I try to refrain from acting like a kid on Christmas morning. He sits on the bed and says, "Let me check the score to this game just real quick," as he turns on the TV.

Not knowing what to do, I go in the restroom and tuck my bag into the corner. I walk back out then Nate pats the bed and signals for me to come sit next to him. I'm nervous.

I sit beside him.

He pulls me closer and laughs.

"I don't bite." He leans in and kisses my neck. "Well, unless you want me to."

I feel goosebumps rise from my skin. Sweet Jesus, he is hot.

After a couple minutes of closeness, he pulls back and says, "You're gonna get me all hot and bothered before dinner. We have reservations in about ten minutes."

I jump up, half relieved, half disappointed.

"Oh, I need to change real quick then."

I go into the bathroom and start to freshen up from the car ride. The black dress I borrowed from Cass is perfect. Despite the awkward distance between us, and the million questions I had to answer (and lie about), it was all worth it. It's the right combination of classy and sexy, and when I slip it on I don't feel seventeen. I put on some strappy heels, and I totally feel like a grown up. I spray body spray onto my neck, touch up my makeup, and let down my hair.

When I walk out of the bathroom, Nate whistles at me, and I love this. I love everything about it. He goes in the restroom for a quick change himself, and when he walks out I almost die. He's gorgeous. A dress shirt, slacks, and cologne. Really good smelling cologne.

"You're a hottie, Nate Bradley." We kiss again.

When we get back on the elevator, Nate pushes the floor button, fourteen, and we ride all the way up to the top of the building. When the door opens, it looks like we've been transported someplace far, far away from the casino.

It's totally fancy.

A live pianist plays in the entryway, and a hostess stands at an illuminated stand. My first thought is, thank God I borrowed the dress from Cass. It would have been so embarrassing to walk into this place in boots and jeans.

Nate reaches for my hand, and we walk in.

The hostess looks up.

"Hi, Mr. Bradley."

I giggle.

"Hey, Felicia."

She reaches for two menus that look like expensive binders, and says, "Right this way."

We enter the dining room, and I feel like Cinderella. You can see the Tulsa skyline through the big windows, and the sunset is beautiful. I can't believe this is real. The sound of plates and silverware, piano and laughter, fill the room—stuff I've only seen on TV.

I look at beautiful people everywhere. Delicious smells, bottles of wine, and candlelit tables create the most romantic mood ever. The waitress pulls out our chairs, and we're seated at a table near the windows. It's the most incredible feeling to be here with Nate.

Nate looks at the wine list and asks if I have a preference.

"You pick," I say since I have no idea how to even pronounce half the wine selections on the list.

The server comes to our table and serves us a bottle of champagne, "Compliments of Rick."

I don't know who Rick is, but this makes Nate smile. "Well, you tell Rick thank you, and I'll be finding him before the night's over." The waitress pops the cork and pours us each a glass. Fizzy bubbles almost overflow the glass but recede in perfect timing. It's obvious this isn't the first glass of champagne our waitress has poured. She tells us about the night's special features— both land and sea— and then leaves the table for us to look over the menu.

Nate raises his glass.

"Here's to the most beautiful woman in the room."

I feel myself blush. I raise my glass and clink his.

"And to the hottest guy in the room, for sure."

I hear my phone buzz in my purse. I set my glass down, unzip my purse, and take a glance without actually pulling out my phone.

It's DAD. Shit, DAD!

I silence my phone then excuse myself to the ladies' room. I bend down and check for feet in stalls and see that the coast is clear.

I call Dad back, and he picks up on the first ring. "Where you at, honey?"

"Hey, Dad. I'm at Cassidy's. We've just been catching up on some homework."

Dad takes a minute to respond.

"At Cassidy's, huh?"

"Yep . . . we'll probably start a movie after we finish studying so I'm just going to crash here tonight."

Dad sits on the line. This makes me nervous.

A lady walks in the bathroom and goes straight to a stall.

Finally he says, "Well okay, hon. You girls have a good night. Guess I'll see you in the morning."

"Alright, Dad. See you tomorrow."

I give myself a few minutes for my heart to get back to a normal pace then walk back to the table.

"Everything okay?" Nate asks as he pours himself a second glass of champagne.

"Yeah, it's fine. Just a friend from work calling to get a password."

"Oh. Now you know I have a no-work policy on getaway weekends." He says and raises his glass once more. "Here's to no work and all play."

"I'll toast to that." *Clink.*

I'm tipsy by the time we finish dinner. Some other guy Nate knows sent over a second bottle of champagne, and the next thing I know we've got two empty bottles sitting on our table.

He signs the bill. "Let's go have some fun, shall we?" He stands and reaches for my hand. I stand and realize, *whoa*, maybe a bit more than tipsy.

We're alone in the elevator on the way down, and Nate seizes the moment. He slides his hand behind my neck and kisses me until the elevator comes to a stop. Champagne plus kissing equals have I died and gone to heaven?

The lights have been dimmed in the casino, and there's a definite party-like atmosphere. It's a mecca for entertainment. Right off the main floor there's a club, and we walk in to take a look around. Nate doesn't know the worker, and the guy lets us know that if we want to reserve a booth tonight "It'll be $200." I turn my head the other direction in case the guy sees my face and gets suspicious about my age.

Nate raises his voice so the guy can hear him over the music.

"We're just taking a look around. Probably won't stay." The guy nods his head, and Nate leads me through the crowd to the circle bar that sits in the corner. There's no way I can drink anything else right now. I need to be in control. It takes a few minutes for the bartender to make his way down to us, and Nate takes it upon himself to order me a margarita.

"Thanks," I say when he hands me the tall glass. I take a sip and WOW is it a strong one. He makes small talk with a few people he knows, two really cute girls and a guy from the city. I sip on my margarita as they talk about football scores and who's going to make it to the championship this year. The girls check me out head to toe, and it makes me uneasy. One gives me a super fake smile then turns to watch the crowd on the dance floor. A new song comes on, and it must be her jam because she squeals and grabs her friend's arm to go to the dance floor. Nate doesn't let go of my hand the entire time, and I really like this. Really, really like this.

We walk out of the club and reenter the casino. There's not an unoccupied slot machine in sight, and some of them ring to signal a win. *Ding, ding, ding, ding!*

Nate says, "Let's make our way to the poker room."

I lick a little salt from the rim of my glass. "Lead the way."

We work our way through the crowd. We pass a sports bar with huge TV's, and Nate stops to check the scores. I wonder if he has money on the game, but I make no mention of it.

Beautiful, modern chandeliers hang over a circular bar, and bodies crowd around waiting for a cocktail or cold beer. We walk for fifteen minutes, and I realize we're still not to the end. Finally, we reach a wing attached to yet another restaurant, and we walk through an elegant hallway and come to a set of masculine, ornate doors.

"You wanna play?" Nate asks. "I need to go back in the office. Shouldn't take more than about an hour."

My face feels numb from the drinks, but I'm relaxed and ready to play.

"Sure."

He opens the door for me, and we walk in to the boys' club of all boys' clubs. Heads turn to look at me—is it the dress? So I grab Nate's hand. He knows just about every worker in the room, and despite the long waiting list, I get a table in about two minutes flat. I get dirty looks from a few old codgers standing along the wall. One guy looks at his watch.

Nate walks to the cashier and buys me a tray of chips. He sets them in front of me, squeezes the nape of my neck. "Good luck."

I scooch my chair closer to the table and remove my chips from the tray. Everyone at the table stares at me, something that usually makes me nervous; however, when you're champagne-numb and your date's Nate Bradley, confidence seems to abound. The ante gets to me quickly. I toss in six bucks before even looking at my hold-cards. I pull up the corners of my cards and try not to react to my killer down-cards. Two aces.

I look behind me and realize that Nate has seen a friend. They chat for a while then he comes back to my table to let me know he'll be back in a few. "No problem," I say and watch him walk out of the poker room. I get fuzzy all over again thinking about being here with him.

I'm hot on the table. I take down the first two pots, and this causes a couple of guys to mutter obscenities under their breath. I like it.

For almost an hour they try to bully me with high bets, which definitely works in my favor. There's a guy across the table that looks to be in his sixties—but trying to be in his twenties—and he's all but declared war. He's wearing a snug Abercrombie t-shirt and is likely some hair club's number one customer. Every time I bet he jumps in and raises, raises, raises. So far, it hasn't worked out for him at all. This has pissed him off to the point that he is throwing his cards after he loses. Wah, wah, wah, big baby. Any time a male's ego shows up on the poker table it's a good thing. My stack is huge.

Could life get better?!

The cocktail waitress comes around to take orders, and the guys at my table put her to work. The last one to order, a bearded guy in a flannel, requests a pear cider beer (would have never guessed that one) then the waitress looks at me like it's my turn. "Can I get you something, sweetie?"

I look down at my cards.

"Uh, sure."

"What'll it be?" She waits with her pad and pen.

"I'll take a . . ." I can't get it out. "I'll take a beer."

She squint her eyes and smiles—sweet, in a fake way. "What kinda beer?"

I'm trying to focus on my hand and sound mature at the same time. "I'll take one of those pear beers too."

The bearded guy approves and talks about how good they are—says his buddies give him a hard time because they're girlie drinks but he doesn't care.

The cocktail waitress disappears.

We play a couple of more hands. I take down a decent one. Mid-life Crisis Guy's not happy, to say the least. He's

1. mad I'm taking his money and 2. mad about time and the natural aging process.

The waitress returns and leans in to deliver each drink, and everyone politely tips her with poker chips. She gets around to me and before she leans in, Mid-life Crisis Guy mumbles loud enough for me to hear.

"I'd check her ID if I were you."

I freeze.

He says it louder a second time.

"Check her ID. I don't even think she's old enough to be in here." He leans back in his chair and takes a sip of his cocktail.

I take a drink of my beer before I set it on the table. The cocktail waitress gets distracted from a guy at another table hollering an order then looks back at our table. I look at my cards and act like I didn't hear a word he just said.

He's planted the seed, and I feel the other players begin to look at me.

Shit.

"Check her damn ID!" He says again.

The cocktail waitress rolls her eyes but appeases him. "Do you have it on you?" she asks. "Louie wants to make sure you're legal when he tries to pursue you later tonight."

This makes the other guys at the table laugh. Louie's PISSED.

I start digging through my purse and my animal instincts begin to take over. Fight or flight? Fight or flight?

I turn back around to face her.

"I think my boyfriend has it. Nate Bradley?"

Name-dropping doesn't work. She tells me to go get it

and she'll be back in a few minutes to check it.

I discretely take the large denomination chips from my stack and slip them into my purse.

Mid-life Crisis Guy gets up to go talk to a guy in a suit.

I slip out fast.

FLIGHT.

I trot, in my heels, to a cashiers' window around the corner and get in a line with two others in front of me.

Faster. Faster. COUNT THEIR MONEY FASTER. I look around the corner to make sure no one's coming then back at the cashier to see where she's at in finishing her transaction. Corner. Counter. Corner. Counter.

The customer folds some cash and stuffs it into his back pocket. The next customer moves up to the counter.

Corner. Counter. Corner. Counter.

I move up in line and set my chips on the counter.

Corner. Corner. Corner.

The cashier moves in slow motion to count my money and fan it across the counter.

Mid-life Crisis Guy comes around the corner and looks around but doesn't see me. A worker follows behind him.

I swoop up the cash as fast as I can and run to the nearest bathroom to hideout and regroup. The last stall is open. I take it.

Shit! Shit! SHIT!

My hands and knees are jolting. Trauma-level panic.

FLIGHT.

I leave the bathroom, trot through the casino, and exit into the parking garage. Cameras. Don't forget the cameras. I try not to bring attention to myself, and walk through the garage to find the nearest exit. It leads to a parking lot, and I step out to get my bearings. There's a Taco Mayo in the distance, two large parking lots over, and I fast walk to make it over there.

It's almost closing time—chairs on tables—and I get a dirty look from the worker when I walk in.

"I'm not eating, can I just use your restroom really quick?"

The worker doesn't reply, she just returns to her closing duties.

I go to the bathroom and squat in the corner to regroup.

Nate.

I start crying.

My wonderful weekend.

I cry some more.

I close my eyes as tears run down my face. Thoughts zoom through my head. I check my phone to make sure Nate hasn't called looking for me, and there's one missed call: Nate.

I'm panicked when I think about me mentioning his name to the cocktail waitress. Would they put it together? Find Nate and tell him what happened? Shit. Surely not.

I'm beyond screwed.

I think of a million ways to try and wiggle out of this so I can return to the casino, but I know I can't risk it.

I'm in Tulsa.

Walking home is not an option.

There's a knock on the door. The worker hollers on the other side. "Ma'am you're going to have to leave. We're closed now."

"Ok, thank you. I'll be out in just a minute." I holler

back.

I pull out the cash from the casino. It's all a blur, and I couldn't have even told you how much I have before I count it.

$250. I hate the fact that I had to leave some on the table and wonder how much it was.

I stand and stuff it back into my purse. I take off my heels and hold them with one hand. Couldn't care less about the dirty floors because there's no way I could take another single step in those things because my feet hurt so badly. The worker is waiting to let me out so she can relock the door.

"Thank you," I say as I walk out. She doesn't respond.

I take a step off the curb and look back at the casino.

Don't cry.

Don't cry, damnit.

I start walking toward a gas station. What the hell am I going to do now?

The street is busy so I walk along the curb. This time I hear my phone ring . . . it's Nate, again. It rings for an eternity.

I keep walking, avoiding glass and random street stuff such as beer cans and a diaper. Cars zoom past me. Two of them honk. I get to the gas station, a busy one, and when I walk in the clerk hollers for me to put on my shoes. It's one of those gas station/mini fast food places. Pain. I force one blistered foot in at a time then wobble over to a booth that's occupied by an old man because all the others are filled with groups.

"Do you care if I sit here for just a second?"

"Go ahead," he replies then wads up a candy bar wrapper and leaves. My phone rings, Nate again, and I don't answer. I worry that he'll find someone to replace me . . . meet someone new . . . since I can't go back.

I think of a million ways to dig myself out of this hole.

No way that I'm calling Cassidy to come get me.

I'd call Ms. Stella, but I don't think she should be on the roads alone this late.

No way in hell I'm calling Dad.

There are a couple of truck drivers meandering around the store. But no. Just, no.

I cry. Some more.

If I had a smart phone I could Google cab companies. At this point I feel so damn sorry for myself I buy a bag of popcorn and eat the whole thing. Why me?

After an hour of contemplating, I get up and ask the clerk if he knows of any cab companies in the area.

"Are you okay?" He asks in a gentle way. He's wearing a baseball cap, and for some reason I trust him.

I pull my hair into a low knot.

"Yeah, I'm fine." I lie.

"Where are you trying to go?"

"Back to Oklahoma City." I hold back tears.

"Yeah, I can call you a cab." He pulls his smart phone from his back pocket and starts the search.

I take my shoes off and stand right beside them and wait a couple of minutes while he Googles around swiping his index finger across his screen. "Looks like it'll be at least a couple hundred bucks." He's sympathetic.

I don't think twice. "Call 'em. I've got it."

As I wait, I decide it would be best if I text Nate. I don't want him to worry about my safety, and I certainly don't need him filing a missing person's report or something crazy like that.

"I'M OKAY. HAVE EMERGENCY AT HOME. WILL CALL YOU TOMORROW."

He immediately responds, "???????????????????"

I'm scared when I get in the cab.

The car isn't marked very well . . . just a number across the outside of the door that's been put on by those big gold stickers.

It's shady.

The guy doesn't say anything to me at all since he already knows we're headed to Oklahoma City. The car smells like something I've never smelled before—a weird combination of cigarette smoke and black licorice. He pushes buttons on a mini-computer meter, and I watch the dollars and cents increase as we merge onto the highway. My phone rings. It's Nate. I silence the ring and just stare at the casino as we pass it. My phone lights up again—Nate. I lean my head against the glass and squeeze my phone. Goodbye, Tulsa.

It's four in the morning when the cab driver drops me off at my car that I left parked at Nate's. I fight back tears when I look over at his apartment.

I pay the driver, which takes most all of my winnings, and then grab my heels that I'd kicked off on the floorboard.

"Thanks," I say.

He grabs the money in a rush and speeds off.

183

I climb into my car, still in disbelief of how this night ended. I sit for a few minutes trying to figure out how to kill about five or six hours before it's logical that I go home. A young girl sleeping in her car in a parking lot would look suspicious, and the last thing I need is some cop questioning me. So I drive to Ms. Stella's, the one person who won't ask questions.

I turn my headlights off before I pull into her driveway, and decide I'll just stay in my car and sleep in her driveway. I grab a hoodie from my back seat, ball it up as a makeshift pillow, and lay my head on my console. I shift around for ten minutes, and with each move I'm reminded of how much this sucks.

♥

I'm awakened by a knock on my window, and you would've thought there was a killer with a butcher knife standing outside my car the way I jumped.

It's Ms. Stella in her robe, her hair a mess. She knocks again. "Chandra, what are you doing out here?" She says loud enough that I can hear her through the window.

I open my car door and she sticks her head in.

"What in the world?"

"Oh, hi Ms. Stella." I put my palm on my heart to slow the pounding. "I'm sorry, I got really tired and couldn't go home."

She doesn't ask why.

"Well get yourself in here, Miss Priss." I fumble around and follow her to her door. The sun is barely starting to show itself; there's a fog covering her lawn.

She goes to the kitchen and starts banging pots and

pans around then pulls a carton of eggs from the fridge. I look at my phone. Five missed calls from Nate.

Ms. Stella makes small talk, but it's so hard for me to concentrate. Thoughts of Nate swirl in my head, and I wonder what he did last night, and what he thinks.

She puts a full plate of breakfast in front of me, and I stare at a single fresh rose in a vase as I eat on her breakfast bar. When I finish, it's still too early for me to go home.

Ms. Stella points to the throw on the back of her couch.

"You go back to sleep, hon." She disappears for a moment then returns with a real bed pillow so I don't have to use the throw pillows on her couch.

I take my plate to the sink and start rinsing. "I'll get that," she says.

Ms. Stella leaves the room, and I nest on the couch. Heaven.

A single tear drips off my nose and no matter how comfortable I feel, I just can't fall asleep. I lie there for a few hours but only doze off for a few minutes here and there.

I decide to be proactive. The faster I resolve this shit-storm, the better.

Right before I get up, I shoot Nate a text:

"MY DAD WAS HOSPITALIZED FOR CHEST PAINS LAST NIGHT BUT TURNS OUT HE'S OK. I DIDN'T WANT TO RUIN YOUR NIGHT SO I JUST TOOK A CAB HOME WITH MY WINNINGS. TALK SOON. THANK YOU FOR UNDERSTANDING."

I reread it four times before I hit send.

When I get home, it's no surprise that Dad's on the couch watching television. He strikes up conversation, but doesn't take his eyes off the talk show featuring Jack Hanna and a little exotic monkey.

"Hey Chels. Do you know what happened to my gun? I was going to take it up to that gun show and try to sell it, but I can't find it."

I freeze and widen my eyes. He's still not looking at me. "Uh, I don't know. Did you check your closet?"

He twists around to face my direction. "It's not in the corner where I usually keep it."

"Then I don't know, Dad," I holler back as I walk to my room, "have you checked the attic?"

He hollers back down the hallway, "Why would it be in the attic?"

"I don't know." I close my door.

Shit. I've got to go get that gun back tomorrow.

One minute later, he opens my door.

"Chels, you don't have any idea where that gun is?"

I look him straight in the eyes. "No, Dad. How would I know where it is?"

He scrunches his nose.

"I just think it's weird that it disappeared all of a sudden." Dad stands there, with sweat pants and hair that hasn't been washed or combed all day. His face looks older today; it's the gray tint of his whiskers.

I reiterate, "Well I don't know where it is."

Dad scratches his head, and I don't know if the scratch is warranted because he's perplexed or because his scalp itches. He glances around my room, as if the gun could be in here.

"I'll find it tomorrow. It's gotta be around here

somewhere." He walks out and closes my door.

My brain quickly devises a plan: On Monday, go to morning classes. Get the gun at lunch. Go back for afternoon classes. But how will I get it in the house? Dad is always at home now. Always.

I'll stick it in my trunk until after school. I'll figure it out somehow. I'm not stressed. I have this gift lately of making things magically happen.

I sit up, but lean back against my pillow and make a to do list for tomorrow:

-Get the gun
-Finish accounting packet
-Go pay electric
-Look for job (always on my list)
-Laundry
-Clean out car

The list gets me straight with the world. Everything's in order.

I hear Dad cracking up. There's probably another monkey on TV or some shit like that. I get under the covers and close my eyes. I think of Nate for a few minutes then I fall asleep. I sleep hard and peacefully. The kind of sleep when you don't even think you dream.

Chapter 30

It's hard to get out of bed for school. I'm not used to a night of blissful slumber, and I just don't want it to end.

Dad doesn't get up to wake me up any more. I'd guess he doesn't even get out of bed until elevenish. This is what happens to people who stay up until three in the morning watching exotic monkeys on television.

I wait until the very last possible minute, and at 7:15 I finally get up and get moving. I have to rush around, but that extra ten minutes of stillness makes it worthwhile.

The bad thing about not arriving to school at a decent time is you wind up with a sucky parking space. Waaay out in the back. I weave in and out of the rows of cars, hoping for a miracle. Just when I think I've won the lottery—an empty space—I realize a champagne colored Mercedes SUV is double parked. I'm irritated that people are driving such high-end cars to school, and that they think they deserve two spaces instead of one. Without a choice, I drive to the second-to-last row and park. I grab my bag, my to do list off my console, and do a brisk mall-walkers walk to the building.

When I walk through the doors I check the digital clock to find I have two minutes before the tardy bell rings. I don't need anything from my locker so I continue the fast walk to first hour. It's Rayna, a cheerleader, who stops me in the hall first.

"Well that was fast!" She says as she looks down toward my foot. Her eyebrows are raised. I'm confused. She elaborates, "Must have been a miracle doctor to heal your foot so fast."

I forgot to put on the damn boot!

I shift my weight and lift my foot off the ground, remembering it was the left one that's injured. "I . . . He . . . I . . . My doctor said that I need to take off the boot some while it heals."

She's hateful.

"Why?!"

I give it my best.

"Because, well . . . because if I wear the boot constantly it may damage the muscles in the arch of my foot."

She laughs sarcastically.

"Huh. Well I've never heard of that before."

A few stragglers left in the hallway begin to pick up speed and run. Beeeeeeep.

I'm tardy.

Another cheerleader, Leslee, joins us. "Where's your boot?" She asks point-blank.

I roll my eyes and start hobbling toward the door. I hobble all the way back out to my stupid second-to-the-last-row car, open the stupid trunk, and grab my stupid boot. I put it on and Velcro the straps, then grab my STUPID crutches. This is so damn stupid.

I hobble through my morning wondering how I'm going to deal with this for four more weeks.

When the lunchtime bell rings, I go all the way back out to my car. There are a million people squeezing into shiny cars together. Groups of kids are laughing, talking, and gathering around being social. For most of them, their biggest concern in the world is what combo they will order at lunch. I, on the other hand, will skip eating to retrieve a gun and, if time allows, swing by and pay the electric bill. This makes me crave a burrito.

But, like always, I take care of business. Gun—check. Electric bill—check.

When I pull back in at school I have plenty of time to get a good parking spot and wobble down the walkway. When I reach the door I look back and notice the police are here with their K9's. Just a normal day of high school . . . something they do a few times a month.

All the blood rushes to my head when I think about there being a gun in my trunk.

I know they're here for drugs, but can they sniff out weapons?!

It all plays out in my head.

Expelled.

Handcuffed.

Sent to jail.

Nate sees my mug shot on the news.

I look out the window and watch my car for a few minutes as they start unloading the dogs.

Should I leave? I'd look guilty of something if I left.

I should leave.

No.

Surely they can't sniff out weapons.

Or can they?

My story if I get detained: It was a family heirloom that I inherited and forgot to take out of my trunk.

No . . . My dad went hunting this weekend and must've forgotten to take it out.

I can see the media circus now: "Police Find Shooter Just in Time." With my picture.

God help me.

I turn around and walk to class hoping, PRAYING, that a dog can't sniff out a rifle.

I get to fifth hour feeling like I've somehow escaped death row until my teacher, Mr. Daggs, calls me to his desk.

He looks over his glasses to read his computer monitor then looks back at me. "Chelsea, they need to see you in the office."

My knees go weak. I can't breathe. "Okay."

I walk slowly out the door. I can't help but start crying when I get to the hallway. I stop in the bathroom to collect myself, and the thoughts won't go away. Mug shot, police car, my dad trying to convince the officers that it's all a big mistake—his girl wouldn't do anything like this.

I blow my nose then wet a paper towel and place it on the back of my neck. I sit on the floor for a minute until I think it's safe to stand without passing out.

I go to the office and look through the glass windows as I open the door.

It's relatively quiet, and I walk to the front desk. Mrs. Messerli, the attendance secretary greets me with a smile.

"Hi. Whatcha need?"

"I'm Chelsea." I look around for uniforms and badges.

She looks around at all her sticky notes scattered across her desk calendar.

"Chelsea. Chelsea. Let me see . . . oh, yes. Your first-hour teacher recommended we give you a special parking pass due to your injury. She said you were tardy today."

I look at her. For a second, I can't find words. "Oh, yes." Tears stream down my face. "That would be great."

Chapter 31

When I get home Dad is horizontal on the couch. Same whiskers, same messy hair, same everything.

I take charge of the situation. I don't know what else to do.

"Dad, I got the gun."

This gets his attention, and I steal him from his beloved *Ellen* show.

"What?" He even hits the mute button.

"Dad, I didn't know how to tell you, but I had pawned the gun to pay a bill. It's just something I had to do, and I should have just told you. I'm sorry, Dad."

Deep down, I want this information to hurt him. I want to light a fire. Let's get something going! Will this register with him? My daughter had to pawn a gun to pay a bill?! Gee, I better look for a job so this doesn't happen again!

He looks back at Ellen, still muted.

"You shouldn't have done that, Chels. Those places are dangerous." He's calm. Too calm.

I can't help myself.

"Yeah, well you didn't leave me with much of a choice." I walk out the door, get the gun, then come back in and place it on the coffee table in front of him. He gives Ellen her voice by clicking the remote—the studio audience bursts into laughter—and that's that.

I go to my room and close the door.

I feel the need to call Cassidy, but she's so far removed from where I'm at this particular moment, she wouldn't understand. I want to call Nate. But what would I say? I get under my covers and try to force a nap, but I can't sleep.

At this point there's an awkward tension between Dad and me, someplace we've never been before. He needs a job. He knows I know he needs a job. He knows I know you don't find jobs lying on the stupid couch all day. I put on my baseball cap, grab my coin purse, and head out the door.

Dad perks up.

"Where are you going?"

"Out." I leave without giving him the chance to respond.

I get in my car without any idea as to where I'm headed. I just drive. Mostly in neighborhoods, where families are doing family things all together as big happy families. A mom sits with her daughter drawing on their driveway with sidewalk chalk . . . A dad throws a bat bag into the back of his car as his son climbs in the passenger seat. An old guy waters his flower bed by hand. I get lost in my thoughts and just keep driving.

It's almost by default that I end up where I do. My car just goes there.

I need to see Nate. But even more, I need to play poker.

I bite the inside of my mouth, but I don't cry when I pull into the parking lot. Inevitably the rent will be due in a week. I don't want to sell my car.

I park under a light, then sprint up toward the building. The smell of smoke is extra strong. I smell it at least ten steps before I even enter the front doors. A calm comes over me when I walk in, and I know this is my night. Some days I feel it, some days I don't. Tonight, I feel it.

I go straight to the poker room.

When I approach the check-in counter the thought crosses my mind that I already don't want it to end. A perfect life would be to just hang around here and play poker. Forever.

Although I only have $100 to get started, I go ahead and take a seat at the high-stakes table. I recognize only one player, and I'm shocked to see Ms. Stella on this table. She must have hit it big on a slot machine or something to be running with the big dogs.

"Well there she is." She winks and gives me a thumbs up.

"Here I am." I laugh politely and unfold my $100 bill to lay out on the table. "Five dollar chips, please." I'm already being dealt in, and I repress the thought that I'm basically playing to keep my car.

My first hand sucks. My second hand sucks, but I haven't lost a dime because it's not my turn to be the blind. Yet.

I sit through five bad hands, and I hope this isn't a sign of what's to come. However, I do like the mojo at this high-stakes table better than the other night. The people are chatty and friendly. They smile in the warmest way as they merge others' chips with their own.

I finally get some down-cards I can work with, and I'm relieved to finally see the royal couple. King and queen . . . like meeting up with old friends after spending time away. I bet to stay in the hand, and then it gets ugly.

A large man with a reddish ponytail goes all in before we even get the flop.

This would be my entire stack.

I can't do it. Not before the flop. I know he's bullying me, but I picture my car in my head then throw my cards back to the middle.

This pisses me off. All in before the flop?! What a bully.

I glance around and come to the realization that Nate must not be working tonight which is okay by me, actually better for me, because I can't be distracted when I've got so much at stake.

I sit through about two hours of the back-and-forth . . . Up a little, down a little . . . then I take down a pretty decent pot, about $400, give or take a few.

This puts me in a much better position. I'm not at their mercy anymore.

$400 would put a serious dent in our rent, but it's just not enough to solve all the problems.

I keep going . . .

Until I'm up $1200 dollars.

Twelve hundred! This would temporarily solve our problems . . . I should really get up. I could tell Dad that I've been working and getting sales commission somewhere . . .

But I keep going.

My imagination runs wild with the possibility of doubling my $1200. And I convince myself it's not even unrealistic to turn my stack into $5000 if I'm patient enough.

I check my phone for the time. 8:24 p.m. Casinos, strategically, do not have clocks on the walls, nor do they have windows. It could be raining poker chips outside and no one in this joint would ever even know. We're in our own, secluded world, not even knowing if it's daytime or night. We're dealt the cards. I pull the corners back and take a peek at mine.

"Hey, come get a bite with me." A hand touches my back.

I turn around to see Nate.

Then look back at my cards.

He waits.

I've got this happy/nervous/I'm-so-glad-to-be-near-him-again feeling. Nate stands behind me, wordless, while I finish the hand. Poker etiquette 101.

After the hand, Ms. Stella lets everyone know that it's getting close to her bedtime . . . she's in for one more hand . . . make it a good one. However, it's time for a dealer change, and Granny can't bear to sit here through the shuffling, counting, and tucking of the money. "Well, I'm out of here. You kids have a good night," she says, then stands.

Nate stays put. Hand on my back.

I stand with Ms. Stella and turn to Nate, "I'd love to," I smile and cock my head, "be right back."

I walk Ms. Stella safely to her car the whole time thinking about how relieved I am that the Tulsa fiasco didn't ruin things for me and Nate. After all, he's here, wanting to talk. That's a good thing. Right?

I go back in and meet Nate in a booth that's tucked in a corner of the sports bar. He looks super hot . . . He tells me I look beautiful and grabs my hand across the table. I'm relieved that he's bought the lie about Tulsa. Things seem okay between us, but I have a twinge of guilt when he asks how my dad's doing and if there's anything I need. "He's feeling much better, thanks though."

"So, what happened?" He looks me dead in the eyes, and I start twisting the end of a paper napkin.

"Just what I said. He had chest pains and went to the emergency room."

He pauses. "Did they find a blockage? Does he have to have surgery?"

"No, he's fine."

"Really? They didn't find *anything*?"

This conversation needs to end.

"Nope." I get snippy.

He can tell I don't want to talk about it so he changes the subject. We talk about other things for a few minutes then he goes back to work.

I go back to the poker table and sit down, then take one chip from my stack and use my pointer finger and thumb to spin it around in circles while the dealer does his thing.

At first I don't pay much attention, but when I look up to see if the game's about ready to start I realize the dealer looks familiar . . . I think he's been my dealer here before. Hair that'd be curly if it wasn't cut so short and eyelashes that extend longer than the average guy's. A pretty boy, in a not-so-stylish way. Probably in his forties. He claps his hands once, and shows the cameras in the ceiling that they're empty and says, "Good luck gentlemen." When he realizes that I'm at the table he adds, "Good luck to you too, little lady." He does a double take.

I look away.

Has he dealt me a losing hand before? There's some type of connection here, but I can't figure it out.

A friend of Nate's? I wonder if Nate has pointed me out to him before. It's completely obvious that he's trying to figure it out too, because he deals the cards in all directions and never takes his eyes off me.

At this point, I'm completely uncomfortable, but what the hell am I supposed to do with over $1000 worth of chips sitting in front of me?

He's not shy, and asks me point blank.

"You play here a lot?"

I look up like I don't realize he's talking to me.

"Oh, me? Yeah, I guess . . . Well, not really a whole lot. Just sometimes." I don't even make sense to myself.

He keeps dealing and chatting.

"Hmm. You just look familiar. I've probably just seen you around here before."

"Yeah, probably." I want this conversation to end. Although I'm sitting with a crappy hand, I look intensely at my cards and try to send him a signal to stop bugging me while I'm focusing on my game. I even go as far as to call my crappy hand so I don't have to toss in my cards and continue this conversation.

I feel him looking at me.

I just stare at my cards.

It must've been crappy cards all-around, because the entire table ends up folding, and I wind up with a small pot to add to my growing stack.

I tell myself just three more hands then I must go. I hope for good cards; I really don't want to sit here through three hands and not participate.

There's still awkward static between the dealer and me, and I try to catch a glimpse of him when I know he's not looking at me. He tosses us our cards, and I barely bend up the corners—one at a time—to take a look at mine. Ace. Ten.

I'll take it.

The entire table calls, and there's already a nice little pot in the works. I look at the dealer's nametag, David, but it doesn't ring a bell. He reveals the community cards, one at a time, and before the last one is even turned face-up, a guy in a hoodie pulled over his head goes all in.

Are you kidding me? I haven't even had time to process the cards, and he's already gone all-in? Intimidation tactic? Or total confidence in his hand?

I'm worried. But not too worried when I see I already have two pair. Aces and tens!

The dealer tilts his head and counts to count the guy's chips, then says, "$900 to call."

Are. You. Kidding. Me.

Nine hundred dollars to stay in this hand?! I squirm in my chair. This is the big one I've been waiting for.

Two others, before me, call the hand and there's $2700 just waiting for the taking. My heart goes berserk, and I'm not the only one trembling. I stare down making sure I'm holding what I think I'm holding. My eyes dart back and forth from the cards in my hands to the community cards on the table. Ace in my hand. Ace on the board. Ten in my hand. Ten on the board. Yes, I confirm, I have it.

I count out $900 and push my chips to the middle. I do it quickly, like ripping off a bandage or plucking a hair.

I get the familiar poker high, and let the hand play out. Additional cards don't help my hand; I end with a strong two-pair.

It's a feeling of being whacked in the stomach with a baseball bat when the guy in the hoodie flips over his diamond flush. It comes from nowhere. I didn't even realize there were three diamonds on the board!

My throat tightens. I get up and start quickly walking to the door.

I feel like I'm going to get sick so I start running to the bathroom. I bolt in, go straight to a toilet, and kneel down without even shutting the stall door.

A loudmouth, who I didn't even get a good look at, brings attention to me as I start dry-heaving in the toilet. She laughs and says, "Ohhhh, honey. Been there done that! Just last weekend! What'd you drink?"

I don't answer. I reach for toilet paper to clean my mouth.

I can tell she's getting closer by the sound of her voice. "Vodka? Tequila?" It's a southern drawl like no other. "It was Cape Cods that did it for me. I puked pink liquid for at least five hours straight and swore I'd never do it again." She sets her bottle of beer on the top of the toilet paper holder as if she's going to help do something.

I flush the toilet and lift myself up.

"I'm okay. Thanks. Really."

She grabs her beer and takes a drink.

"Take care of yourself. It's awful early in the night to be bowin' down to the throne."

I feel no need to explain to this woman that I haven't

been drinking. I go to the sink and wash my hands. I look in the mirror at my own reflection to see a girl in a baseball cap with watery eyes, and I quickly look back down and begin splashing water on my face.

I can't find Nate to say goodbye, but it's for the best. I don't want him to see me like this anyway. I text him a goodnight message, and he does the same.

I lie in bed that night, unable to sleep, reliving the hand over, and over, and over again. How did I miss the three diamonds?

The next day, I stay home from school. Again. Dad doesn't even realize I'm still home until around eleven when I come out from my room for some milk. "What are you doing here?"

"I live here." I say in a smart-ass tone.

"Why aren't you at school?"

"I'm sick." I pour my glass of milk and return back to my room.

He has no other questions and assumes his position on the couch. I surely have nothing to say.

It's his fault.

All of it.

The stack of unpaid bills . . . the casino . . . the loss . . . everything. It's all his fault.

I get back under the covers because I don't know where to go from here. I don't want to sell my car. I don't want to be in high school. I don't want to be Chandra to Nate . . . but I can't be Chelsea to Nate. Ever.

I sleep all afternoon.

Chapter 32

I stay home for two more days and hardly leave my room. Nate's called twice, but I don't answer and I don't return his calls.

When I finally pull myself from the confines of my bed, I do laundry because I'm down to my last clean pair of anything. Dad keeps his distance, and that's fine by me.

I tell myself I can work out of this. I'll try again.

I leave the house with fifteen dollars in my purse.

And I go back.

When I go in, I feel different. I feel dirty.

There's a waiting list for the low-stakes table. I add my name, seventh on the list, and walk around. I walk slowly because I can't shake the feeling of dread.

I sit down at a slot machine, not to play, just to sit. I look down the row of bright machines all chanting their own enticing lures.

"Wheeeel of Fortune!!!" *Ding, ding, ding, ding, ding, ding!* Lights flashing, the machines sit patiently, just waiting to be fed.

At the end of the row an elderly man sits down, pulls some crinkled cash from his back pocket, smoothes a bill, and feeds the machine.

He plays, intensely, leaning close to the machine to get the best view. He pushes the button. Over and over and over again, and nothing lights up . . . no bells ring.

He stops and leans back in his chair.

He pulls another bill from his crinkled wad, smoothes it over his leg, then feeds the machine again.

I can't watch.

I get up and leave.

I'm almost to the exit door when Nate gently grabs my elbow and turns me toward him.

He's working; I can tell by his suit jacket.

"Hey, where ya been lately? I've been trying to call," he says.

I squint from the sunshine coming from the window and fake a quick smile. "Oh, sorry. I've been sick."

"Blood sugar again?"

What is he talking about?

"No . . . I think it was a sinus infection or something like that. Just stuffy head and a little achy." Then I remember about the whole blood sugar thing.

"Oh. Well, I've been missing you."

I look at him for a longer-than-usual moment. "Look, I don't want to get you sick. I'll just call you when I start feeling better, okay?"

"Are you sure you're okay? Is something going on?"

I stand, speechless. And for one second I want to tell him everything. Start to finish. I want to say it all. I want to tell him that my mom left when I was only six. I want to tell him that I haven't been taken care of since. That I go to high school where everyone has stuff and cars and parents who hold down good-paying jobs with insurance. I want to tell him that my name is not Chandra, and I live in a house the size of a walk-in closet. That I pawned a gun to play poker. I want to tell him that soon I'll be evicted. I want to let him know that when I play poker I'm a million miles away and I love the way that makes me feel.

But I don't.

I don't tell him anything. I barely smile, shrug my shoulder, and shake my head to say, "No."

I walk into the bright sunshine.

And I don't go back.

Chapter 33

For two weeks I don't step foot in the casino because I attempt to do better. I work hard at school. I put my application in at three different restaurants and one clothing store. I deep-clean the house and keep up the laundry. I spend extra time at Miss Stella's . . . I even start eating fruit.

I'm very aware that all these things are not for the betterment of my character, rather, I am punishing myself for the horribly stupid loss of that one single hand that I just can't seem to shake. How could I be so inattentive? His hand was practically screaming out to me "Back off, you idiot! It's a flush!" But I just didn't hear the scream. As simple as that.

With one more week of the boot, I feel it's believable enough that I can now put pressure on my foot. No more crutches. I imagine myself at the tip of the Titanic leaning over—one crutch in each hand—and chucking them into the deep blue. I imagine soaking them with gasoline and dropping a match. Also, in my head, I go after them with an ax.

But I simply wrap them in a towel and place them in my trunk and never think about them again.

It's liberating, to say the least.

So I gather my books and get out of my car with ease, not having to balance on one foot as I prop the crutches to grab the books to hobble away in armpit pain.

Yes, I have bills. And, yes, I am in the middle of the Atlantic without a floatie, but I am making it.

One day at a time; my new motto.

I'm fake hobbling down the hall when it happens.

I don't even have to strain to remember his name.

I look deep into the crowd, and there he is.

David.

Information files rapidly into my brain:

David is wearing a t-shirt and sports jacket.

David is an older man walking amongst teenagers and lockers.

David has a pencil tucked behind his ear.

David, the dealer, is a teacher.

David, the one who knew he knew me, is a teacher!

I divert and crouch behind the moving crowd of kids and speed up my pace. I don't take my eyes off of him, and he never looks my way. He checks his phone as he walks. I slip into my class, unseen. I sit down at my desk, and take my folders out, the bell rings, and I feel like a fugitive in hiding.

I know most teachers have second jobs, but I thought waiting tables or working in department stores was more of the norm. A card dealer?! Really?

This makes me uneasy between passing periods. I must avoid his hall, so I go to the office to check out the directory. DAVID LACKEY, Psychology, room 212. I've heard people talk about Mr. Lackey's class before . . . how awesome he is . . . how they talk about cool stuff and do cool projects . . . but NEVER have I heard someone say he's a teacher by day and dealer by night. I don't think anyone knows this about Mr. Lackey. It seems like this would be an ethical issue, working in a casino. Just like teachers can't be strippers, or can they? Sheesh. Pay the teachers more, already!

Chapter 34

After school, I decide that my self-imposed two-week sentence is enough. And being the gambler that I am, I'm willing to take the gamble on playing again. Yes, there's the Mr. Lackey issue, but I know I'll be fine if I stay on the low-stakes tables. He's never dealt that game before so there's no reason for me to think he'll be dealing that tonight. Besides, leaving right after school gives me an hour or two window. I can't imagine him having to be at work for an evening shift by three-thirty.

I can't get there fast enough. I feel giddy, like being on a diet for two weeks then getting a big slice of red velvet cake. I'm so excited that when I park I run into the yellow concrete bumper, and it jolts me back into consciousness. Calm down, I tell myself. I know better: I'm in no state to play poker, and I decide I must get some composure before I go in.

I sit in the car, take deep breaths, and I hope that I see Nate. Hopefully he's working. Two weeks has been too long, and I realize now that I like him even more than I realized.

I want Nate.

I want poker.

I want a big win.

I take off the boot, toss it into the back seat, and check myself in the mirror. It's one of my better hair days, and I hope Nate is able to see this.

I know that it's basically an all-in situation, and I'm not even at the table yet. I take my waded up ten bucks, two dollars made up of quarters, dimes, and nickels (how embarrassing), and stick it all in my back jean pocket. I take a few more deep breaths, and enter the smoky, adult version of Disney World.

It's that feeling, again. That feeling of being somewhere exotic. The two-week hiatus makes it that much sweeter.

I see Nate before he sees me. But when he does see me at the front sign-up counter, he stops mid-conversation with a dealer. He holds his finger up to the dealer, and I read his lips when he says, "Hang on just a second." He doesn't wait for acknowledgment from the dealer. He doesn't take his eyes off me and walks my direction.

"Well, hello." He says smiling through his words.

"Hi, there," I say.

We're mutually happy to see one another.

"Long time, no talk."

His soapy, clean smell cuts through the casino smoke. I step closer to get more of it. "I know, I'm sorry. I've had so much going on."

His smile grows bigger.

"I've missed seeing you around."

"Well I've missed seeing you too." I put my hands in

my back pockets.

We stare and smile, then smile and stare some more.

"Do you need a table?"

"Yeah. 3-6."

"What, no high stakes today?"

I pull my hair behind my ear.

"Oh, I may make my way over there later. We'll see," I laugh, "I need a warm-up. I'm a little rusty."

He turns to a worker in a suit and says, "By all means, Rick. Let's get the lady warmed up. 3-6."

Rick looks around the room. Then says, "Right this way, ma'am."

I know that Nate knows this is not the end of our encounter, so he walks off confidently, knowing we'll talk again before I leave.

I sit down, super excited to be here but wishing I was on the high-stakes table. Because sometime today someone will take down a big pot that could be mine.

I take out my money and try to make sure the change doesn't make noise as I stack it neatly in one dollar stacks. I don't look at anyone until it's traded out for poker chips. I mean, four quarters wager the same exact way a dollar bill does, right?

I'm the only girl at the table, and none of the players look familiar. A couple of months ago I would have let that intimidate me, but not today. In fact, this is to my advantage because they think I know nothing. I will do everything in my power to let them think this of me, because, after all, the "less I know," the better.

I decide to play it up, just a bit. For fun.

I throw an ante out, knowing that it's not my turn for the blind.

The dealer retrieves it, and tosses it back to me.

"Miss, it's not your blind, yet. I'll let you know when."

The guys all look around at each other and crack smiles letting each other know, in the silent-poker-form-of-communication, that I'm ready for the taking.

I play a few hands without betting. I laugh on the inside when I ask my neighbor, "What makes a flush, again?"

He leans my direction. "It means all the same suit. Like all diamonds, all hearts; you've got to have five of the same suit."

"Ohhh." I nod my head in understanding. "Thanks. I always get a flush and full-house confused."

I take down a few decent pots, and my dumb-blonde-poker-player persona is working nicely until we change dealers, and the dealer calls me by name.

"Hey, Chandra."

The players look at each other. They're all asking themselves how the dealer knows my name. Needless to say, my hamming it up comes to an end. This isn't a bad thing, though, it keeps them guessing, in other words, I'm still a mystery and that's exactly what you want to be to your opponents. A mystery.

We're deep in the middle of a hand when I look up and almost pee myself.

I don't know when he got here, but he did.

Mr. Lackey.

Chapter 35

My eyes shift back and forth, back and forth . . . back and forth . . . from the game to Mr. Lackey's location in the room. He's at a safe distance, but it stresses me out, no doubt.

A pair of queens in the hole temporarily takes my mind off the Lackey factor. I bet heavy, and come out a winner. My stack is growing nicely. The guys at the table think I'm just a dumb blonde getting lucky every once in a while. What they don't know is that I've got them all figured out, but one. Their "tells" include: excessive blinking, shaky hands, knuckle cracking, and cigarette lighting, all independent of one another. It's just another day at the office. After thirty minutes of my stomach growling, I take a break to go get a burrito from the food court.

At the cashier's window I exchange a five dollar chip for the cash, then walk and get in line behind a couple scraping their change to come up with as much as they can. She's digging around at the bottom of her purse; he's checking every pocket in his jeans to make sure he hasn't missed a single coin. Discovering a hidden quarter right now would be like hitting the jackpot.

I overhear their conversation. It's hostile.

"If you wouldn't have played it all back we'd have some to eat on!" She sets her purse on the floor and squats to get in a better digging position. Her khaki capris are in decent shape, but her white canvas tennis shoes have seen better days.

He responds with a sarcastic laugh. He wants to fight. "How do I always get blamed for this?!"

She continues to dig.

I take two dollar bills and hand them to her. "Here. Take this . . . Yes, I'm sure."

They're so very appreciative. One would think that I just ordered them steaks and lobster tail.

"No, really . . . It's no big deal. I'm having a good day," I say.

I hear the couple as they discuss the sum of their loose coin and my donation: $5.37. Then, they step up to the cashier and place their order . . . I'm directly behind them, so of course I hear everything. The lady orders for both of them.

"One burrito, one taco, and two waters."

The cashier punches in the order, and I catch a glance of the digital numbers that light up the total before the lady steps in front of it in effort to conceal it.

$2.01! Their order total is $2.01, and they have no intention of handing me back my money! They scoot down the counter and grab their sack of food with a sense of urgency, and I stand in disbelief.

My anger turns to sadness quickly, because I realize

that they have a serious gambling problem, and there's no doubt in my mind that my two dollars—their last two dollars—will end up in a slot machine. It's so incredibly sad. These people have problems.

I get my burrito, devour it in a few bites, and make sure I top off my Coke before I go back to the table. I purposefully do not look down the rows of slot machines. I do not want to see the couple that just put me together for two bucks. I file the situation in a folder in my brain that I will never open again. There are a couple of empty seats when I return to the table, but chips reserve their place.

I get comfortable in my chair, work my tongue around my teeth to remove the remaining tortilla and bean shells, and survey my stack. I'm consciously aware that life is good with a full belly, a stack of chips, Nate in the building, and cards flying across the table declaring a new hand.

Then, it happens.

Two big-bellied security guards and a woman in a black skirt suit walk over to Mr. Lackey's table. He stops his deal, even stands up mid-hand, and nods my direction. My heart pounds like never before, and I start to feel woozy.

They all look directly at me, and Mr. Lackey nods his head.

The thought crosses my mind to pick up my chips and run for the door, but I become paralyzed. I can't move.

I toss in my cards, out of turn, and slump down in my chair, hoping, PRAYING, that it's not happening.

With the suit lady as their leader and without urgency, they walk straight to me. I know this not by looking directly at them, but by using every capability of my peripheral vision. I know a black blur comes around the table then stops directly behind me.

The lady leans down and whispers in my ear.

"You need to come with us."

My hands are shaking at convulsive levels . . . ironically like the time I took down my first big pot. I don't reply; I just start stacking my chips to take with me, wherever it is I'm going.

The lady leans down again.

"You won't need those. Leave your chips on the table." She is firm, and there's a military aura about her.

I release the chips from my hands.

I know this is it.

I know somewhere that Nate is processing what is happening to me. Is he mad? Does he hate me? Is he embarrassed?

I comply.

We walk through the main walkway of the casino. They don't grab my arm and lead me, nor do they place me in handcuffs. I even get the sense that one of the security guards feels sorry for me.

The ringing of the slot machines sounds muffled. It's all surreal, and I don't even feel like I'm in my own body. I think of Dad, and I stop a tear with my hand before it rolls down my face. My nose becomes runny, and of course I sniffle. We walk in formation: me in the middle, security guards on each side, and the lady behind me. It seems endless, like we're walking across the country.

We enter a door that leads to an area with a couch, kitchen, television, and reclining chairs. There's another security guard kicked back eating a sandwich and watching TV. A walkway separates the living space and the offices, divided only by glass windows.

Still no sign of Nate.

The security guards join their coworker to watch *Wheel of Fortune*, and I realize it's at least six-thirty in the evening, later than I thought.

I'd do anything to be in my living room watching *Wheel of Fortune* with Dad.

I'm still in shock when the lady motions for me to go in her office. "Let's go in here," she says.

She sits behind her desk, and I catch a glimpse of her family photo displaying four kids, a husband, and golden retriever. I'm surprised, because she doesn't come across as the motherly type.

"Have a seat," she commands.

I settle into a cheap plastic chair. I know she knows I'm scared to death. Her hair is pulled up in a stylish way. She pulls paperwork and an old Polaroid camera from her desk drawer. I wonder if the cops have already been called.

"Do you know why you're here?" she asks.

I choose not to respond.

She "Can I see some identification?"

I cry.

I unzip my purse and my shaky hands manage to pull my driver's license from my wallet. I place it on her desk, then scoot back in my chair, as far back as I can go.

She stares at me, almost hesitating, then picks up the plastic card that tells who I am. She only looks at the picture for a second because she has no doubt that it's me.

She puts on her red-rimmed reading glasses, and reads the information aloud.

"Chelsea. Chelsea Knowles." She goes on to read my

birth date, address, weight, and every other detail that the Department of Public Safety finds necessary to include on a driver's license. She sets my license down and folds her arms. "So you're only seventeen?"

I can't answer verbally. I just shake my head yes.

"Well, Miss Chelsea, do you know the legal gambling age in the state of Oklahoma?"

I nod yes, again.

She answers her own question.

"It's eighteen. You must be eighteen-years-old to gamble."

My nose is runny and the tears just keep coming. She surprisingly hands me a tissue.

I look back through the glass windows to see if the real policemen have arrived yet.

The police have not arrived.

But Nate has. He's standing in the hallway with his hands on his hips, staring in our office.

Bad has gotten worse.

Chapter 36

The lady in charge looks around me to see what it was that I just saw that caused more tears.

She sees Nate, says nothing at all to me, and gets up and walks out the door. I turn around again, to see what it is she's doing, and she stands there with Nate talking for a very long time. Is he working in my favor? Or is he so pissed he's requesting maximum penalty? I can't hear a word they're saying, and it's the unknown that's the worst punishment of all.

I have a vision of Cassidy wearing her cheer uniform and visiting me in jail.

I think of Dad the most. What would he do without me? How will he survive? Who will write out the bills? Balance the checkbook?

I sit for eternity, turning around every few minutes. The security guards haven't budged from their original positions, and Nate and the lady just keep talking.

After I've about cried myself sick, she reenters the office.

"Chelsea. Let me explain a few things to you."

I remain silent.

"First, I'm not sure if you realize that this casino is on tribal land . . . meaning, the Cherokee Nation Security has jurisdiction over any criminal penalties. Do you understand?"

I don't understand what this means at all, but I nod my head yes.

Her cell phone rings, she picks it up, answers, and quickly steps back outside her office.

I wait.

I assume that a higher-up has given her a call to discuss my punishment. Jail.

Will they clean out my locker at school? Will I be known as the girl who went from cheerleader to jailbird?

After a few "yeses" and a "that sounds good," the lady steps back into the office and takes a seat back at her desk. She's 90 percent hard-ass, but 10 percent softie. "Chelsea. Underage gambling can be a serious offense." She pauses and takes a drink of coffee from a Styrofoam cup. "However, your friend . . . Nate . . . has assured us that we will never have this problem again. In other words, you walk out that door, and we never see you again. Well, until you're eighteen, anyway." She winks.

I cry more and speak words for the first time.

"Yes ma'am." Sniffle. "I won't come back. I promise."

She reveals her soft side when she hands me a box of tissue and says, "Get outta here."

I grab a few and stand to walk out.

"Thank you. Thank you so much."

I want to hug her.

"Oh, Chelsea. One more thing . . . Stay away from

that Nate friend of yours. He's just bad news when it comes to girls. What do you guys call it? A player?"

My heart sinks.

She goes on.

"Honestly, I don't know how he keeps all of you straight."

Chapter 37

Nate is waiting for me in the hallway. I wipe my nose, look at him, and keep walking. He calls me by my real name for the first time.

"Chelsea? Wait." He catches up to me. "Let's talk about this."

I'm overwhelmed with the events. I don't want to deal with him so I keep walking.

He's angry.

"I think you owe me an apology."

This strikes a nerve.

"An apology? I owe you an apology? For what?"

We continue our conversation while I head for the door.

"For everything. For basically lying to me about your whole entire life . . . Or instead of an apology, how about a 'thank you' for saving your ass." He's hateful.

I keep walking.

He stops. I don't turn around.

I just keep walking.

I have a complete breakdown when I get in my car. I cry hard. Really, really hard. The kind of cry when you can't catch your breath. I grab a tissue from my console and blow my nose then put my key in the ignition.

I'm just about to pull out when Nate walks up and taps on my window.

He uses his pointer finger to request that I roll down my window.

So I turn my key and roll down my window.

"Let's talk about this," he says.

I just look at him like he's crazy. *I don't know how he keeps all of you straight.*

I sarcastically laugh.

"What's there to talk about?"

He walks around to the passenger side and tries to open the door. I unlock it, and he gets in. "We've been dating all this time, and I feel like I have no idea who you even are."

"Yeah, well, the feeling's mutual." I snap back.

"What's that supposed to mean?"

I don't make eye contact.

"It means I have no idea who you are either. How many girls are you dating?"

"Whoa, whoa, whoa. Why are you turning this around on me?"

I hear his question, but I don't respond.

He shifts his body toward me and pauses before he asks, "Where do you even live?"

"I live with my dad. I'm in high school, Nate. Now will you get out of my car?" Another tear drops.

He's stunned.

"High school?" He shifts again, this time facing

forward. "Shit."

He sits in silence for at least a whole minute. "And to answer your question, there's been no one but you. Since the day I first saw you, you've been it." He sits in silence, again, this time even longer. Finally, he takes my hand, kisses it, and gets out of the car.

I watch him as he walks back toward the building. I put my car in reverse. And for the last time, I leave the casino parking lot.

I end up at Ms. Stella's. It's as if my car was on autopilot because when I pull into her driveway, I hardly remember the drive at all. Ms. Stella is pulling her trash can to the curb, so I turn my headlights off and step out of my car. She dusts her hands the way workers do when they complete a big task.

"What a nice surprise," she says. "You're just in time for a midnight snack."

I force a smile.

"What's wrong, dear?" She weaves her arm into mine, and pulls me into her house. I'm sure red eyes and smudged mascara is the giveaway.

I don't respond so she starts guessing.

"Bad night on the table? Pimple? Let me see your face."

I force another smile.

"It's not boy trouble is it? Tell me his name, and I'll go let the air out of his tires."

She scurries to the kitchen and pulls some aluminum foil back off the top of a pan. I sit down at the table. She cuts two pieces of chocolate cake and licks her fingers after each piece.

"I'll tell ya right now. Boys are stupid. The sooner you figure that out, the better." She takes a bite of cake then sits down with me at the table.

I look her in the eyes. For a split second I think about telling her everything. All of it.

But I don't.

I listen to Ms. Stella tell me about the meaning of life. She talks about the struggles we encounter, the highs and lows, and about how some days are diamonds and some days are stones. She talks to me in the most gentle, affectionate way, and I listen. Just listen. My piece of cake goes untouched, so she transfers it to a Tupperware container and lovingly places it in my hands.

"Chin up," she says.

Chapter 38

Despite my efforts to try to conceal it, I know Dad can tell that I've been crying when I walk through the door. He sits up on the couch and uses the remote to turn off the TV. This is an upgrade from the usual muting.

"What's going on, Chelsea. Have you been crying?" He looks me over. Oh, now you've decided to pay attention? I remain silent.

"I don't know what you're talking about," I say finally, while I gauge his expression.

"Don't even try. You've been acting strange." He looks uncertain. Probably thinks I'm just being an irresponsible, rebellious teenager. "Where have you been? I know you've been lying to me."

How would I even talk to him about it? Let's see. Where would I start? I've been trying to make ends meet . . . I have a mad crush on an older guy that I almost spent the night with and will likely never see again. I had to leave a stack of chips on the table that was the equivalent of an electrical bill and rent . . . Bills you couldn't pay because you're oblivious to our financial situation. I sit right beside him on the couch and start pulling my hair up into a knot on the top of my head.

My dad has never had to discipline me. Like everything else, I do this myself. I'm not expecting to get grounded or have some type of punishment. This is not how our house works. But this is worse. He somehow knows I've been up to something, and I hate it. I can't talk myself out of this one.

I weigh my options. Tell the truth? Some of it? All of it? Start small. Breathe in, breathe out.

"I've been hanging out at a . . . casino," I say softly, avoiding his gaze.

"Casino? What were you doing at a casino? Gambling? Meeting someone for drugs?" He's surprised. What was he expecting me to say?

"Drugs? Seriously, Dad?" I stare at him incredulously. Okay, I guess I am going to tell him the whole truth. Minus Nate. He doesn't need to know about that part. "I was playing poker to make some damn money for us, because you sure as hell aren't doing much." I stand up and walk toward the kitchen. Is he really that oblivious?!

"Playing poker? Chelsea, I've been applying for jobs, and I know I'm getting a few calls back this week." His voice calms. "We will get through this rough patch. There's no reason for you to put yourself in danger."

"Dad, enough already! You're not getting any calls back! I know you're not!" I slam my purse onto the kitchen table. *Whack.*

"Listen here, Missy!" His tone grows stern. "You don't come in here talking to me like that. I'm still your father!" He stands and tosses the remote onto the coffee table. "I should be the one hollering at you! Our situation isn't that dire. We will be okay."

I start to walk toward my bedroom. Under my breath, "You're clueless."

He follows me.

"EXCUSE ME? What did you say?"

"I SAID YOU'RE CLUELESS, DAD! You have no idea how many close calls we've had. You have no idea what I have had to do around here to get us through the day! And the next! And the next!" I wave my arms in the air.

This takes him back. He just stares at me.

I want my words back. I don't want to hurt him. I soften my voice.

"I mean, I do a lot, Dad. I was just trying to figure out a way to make it happen!" I have no tears left.

"Chelsea, do you know what goes on in casinos? Drugs! Prostitution! Gangs! God knows what else!"

I look him in the eyes.

"I didn't get hurt, Dad."

"YOU COULD HAVE!" He's yelling again.

I plop down onto my bed and he walks out.

He's almost back to the kitchen when he yells, "YOU'RE GROUNDED."

I half-laugh.

Grounded.

Grounded from what? My life? Because that would be great.

Chapter 39

The next day I call Cassidy. Like a confessional prayer, I tell her everything. Start to finish.

She listens.

I go deep, deep, deep into the story, something I could only do with Cassidy.

She doesn't say much, just listens intensely with an occasional, "Are you serious?"

I give her specifics about the bust, how I thought I was going to jail, and how I can't stop thinking about Nate. I even tell her that I faked my injury to get off the squad. When I finally finish, she's silent for a moment.

"You still there?" I ask.

"I'm here." More silence. I find myself counting the seconds before she speaks again.

"What are you going to do now?" she asks quietly.

"I honestly don't know. Everything is a mess."

I pick up dirty clothes off of my floor. She sighs.

"Chelsea, I'm your best friend, and you know I'm here for you. We can figure this out together. I have some secret cash stashed in my drawer if you need it."

It's the same ole same. Chelsea needs help. Cassidy saves Chelsea.

When we hang up, I glance down at my phone and see a text message notification. What? When did this happen?

It's from Nate. My stomach flip-flops as I open the message and start speed reading.

"Hi. I don't like how things ended. I can't stop thinking about you. You've left me with so many questions. I keep watching the front door in the poker room hoping you'll walk in, but I know you won't. Why did you accuse me of seeing other girls?"

Just as I finish reading, another text comes through:

"Yes I have a past, but I'd like a chance to explain. You are beautiful and I loved spending time with you. I want to know who you really are. Can we meet? Maybe just coffee or something like that? I think we need to talk."

I read them both again.

Then one more time.

Butterflies, butterflies, more butterflies. I wait a minute then text back.

"Yes."

Two hours later, we're sitting across from each other in a crowded Starbucks. Dad has never grounded me before, so when I told him I was going to Cassidy's, he didn't even blink. Typical, oblivious Dad.

I take a drink of my tea and look across the table at Nate.

"Aren't you going to order some coffee?"

He smiles gently. "Nah. I'm not really big on coffee."

I grin and shake my head. "There's tea too, you know."

He smiles, but doesn't say anything. We people-watch for a few minutes before he breaks the silence.

"How are you?" He seems genuinely interested.

"I'm okay." I look away. "Hangin' in there."

Another minute passes.

"How are you?" I ask.

"I'm okay. You know, not much going on. Just work."

It hasn't been long since I've seen him last, but it feels like forever ago. I feel like I have no idea what's going on in his life—like he's a stranger.

"So?" He looks at me expectantly.

"Sooo, what?"

"So, tell me more. Tell me more about Chelsea."

"I've already told you. I'm still in high school. I'm only seventeen."

"Yeah, I know that part." Nate picks up my tea and takes a drink. "But like, where do you live? Where do you go to school? Why were you sneaking into casinos?"

I give him the short version. The truth, just not every detail. I tell him about dad, about cheer squad, about electric bills. I needed money.

He soaks it all in.

"Wow. Brave girl."

"I had to do it, you know? I didn't have a choice."

He nods and looks at me silently for a few minutes, rubbing his hands together uncertainly as if he wants to reach for mine.

My turn.

"So, I hear you're a player, huh?" I ask, laughing a little.

"Yeah, who told you *that*?"

"One of your coworkers."

"No. I am *not* a player." He's serious. "I dated around

a year or two ago. So what? I was young and having fun. But since I've met you, there's been no one else. No one. Promise."

"That's what they all say," I tease.

He gets firm. "Look. I promise you, Chelsea, I haven't talked to anyone since we've been . . . seeing each other."

For some reason, I actually believe him.

"Well, okay." I look him right in the eyes.

We sit there for another hour because we don't want it to end. Nate says he wants to still see me, but he's worried about me being underage.

"I actually had a buddy who got in a lot of trouble for that. He ended up serving time."

"Um, that's not good. I turn eighteen in a few months." I say, looking at him with hopeful eyes.

"Well, I guess we'll just have to wait. I'm glad this relationship isn't over. It's just—"

"Postponed," I laugh.

"Yeah, *postponed*." Nate smiles. Dimples.

Just a few more months and maybe, just maybe, we can finally be something. No lies, just truth.

Chapter 40

Dad shocks the hell out of me two days later when I walk into the kitchen as I'm getting ready to leave for school. He is sitting at the table with a plate of toast and coffee. He is bright-eyed with a clean shave and combed hair. It startles me at first. It's been a long time since I've been greeted by him this early in the morning. He looks up and sees the shock on my face.

"Hi, hon." He says, nonchalantly.

"Uh, what are you doing up?"

He takes a bite of toast and washes it down with coffee.

"I'm starting a job today."

"You're what?"

"I'm starting a job today. It's going to be a good one . . . great benefits, guaranteed base pay, weekends off."

Finally.

I smile.

"You had me at benefits. Where at?"

"Walker Brothers Furniture."

"What are you going to do?"

He chomps on more toast.

"Salesman. I get commission too. And bonuses."

"Wow. I'm really proud of you, Dad."

He stops eating for a second and smiles. He looks at his watch (Dad's wearing a watch?) and gets up to clean his plate. He cups the back of my head, kisses my forehead, says, "See ya tonight, kiddo," and walks out the door.

I stand there, still in disbelief.

I look at the table where he sat.

I look at the dish in the sink to confirm that this really just happened.

I hear the garage door go up and then his truck engine turning over and giving it its best shot. Two more tries. Almost . . . almost . . . His truck starts.

Wow. This is really happening.

As I turn out all the lights and gather my backpack, I'm consumed with wild thoughts of when Dad actually starts bringing home a decent check. My imagination gets the best of me, and I envision us moving into a better house. Everything is painted brightly, no chips in the paint or stains in the carpet. There's even a fluffy dog and picket fence for God's sake. In my daydream, I see my Dad handing me money for lunch, flowers in a flowerbed, and someone spraying fertilizer on the lawn. It's too real.

At school, I'm on a constant look-out for Mr. Lackey in the hallways. Nothing he can do to punish me at school, but nonetheless, I don't want to cross his path. In every single class I am mesmerized by this idea that Dad and I could have this normal, suburban life. In my last period, English, I decide to be proactive and pull out a scratch piece of paper. I list the top five places that I could apply for a job, four of them being restaurants.

After school, I go to the Goodwill to look for a decent job-searching outfit. I walk in, and there's a boy wearing a blue vest, "Goodwill" stamped across the back. His back is to me, and I can't see his face. He's busy. He's busy straightening the shopping carts, perfectly aligning them inside one another, and he is determined that this will be the neatest row of shopping carts a store has ever seen. I don't need a shopping cart, but this catches my attention, so I pause.

He works fiercely with these shopping carts, pulling them out one at a time, making sure not to jam them in a crooked, messed up way.

I can't stop watching. I stare in a trance.

At one point, he bends down and reaches with his hands to straighten a wheel that was pointed to the side. Then he pulls a red cloth from his pocket and dusts the top of the wheel.

Pristine, this row of shopping carts.

He takes one step back, and I can't tell if he's admiring his work or perhaps looking for an unnoticed wheel gone astray. He turns around to find his next task and sees me.

"Welcome to Goodwill!" He smiles enthusiastically, and it's now that I realize he has Down's Syndrome. His glasses fall mid-nose, causing him to point his chin up so he can look through them. He smiles, so passionately, and goes on to tell me that all the blue tags are "half-off" today.

"Thank you," I answer, and return the smile.

He scurries off—a man with a mission—and I walk in slow motion, thinking about this respectable work ethic

I've just witnessed.

I think about his challenges.

His lack of ever having complete independence.

But mostly, I think about his contentment.

I make my way to the skirts, and sift through a million "no's" before I find a "yes." It's a knee-length, black pencil skirt, with the bonus blue tag hanging from the waist. I inspect it top to bottom, and find there's no missing buttons or ripped out seams.

There's a white ruffled dress shirt I find to go with it, and although it doesn't have a blue tag, the original tags from the department store are still attached so I know it's never been worn. Funny how people buy something brand-new and never seem to wear it a single time.

I immediately wash the clothes when I get home. And when they're all dry and pressed, I slip them on, and find immense gratification in knowing that I paid five bucks for an outfit that could probably retail for $100.

Chapter 41

The manager, a middle-aged, redheaded lady glimpses at the front of my application then flips it over to scan the back.

"Can you work Sundays?" she asks as she sets the application aside and starts dropping flour tortillas on a large, flat grill. This question sounds hopeful.

"Yes, I can work Sundays." I watch as she flips at least a dozen puffy tortillas in about three seconds flat.

"You sure? Because I can't tell you how many times someone says they're available on Sundays then, all of a sudden, they mark off every Sunday."

"I'm sure."

She uses the spatula to stack all the tortillas together and move them off the grill.

"When can you start?"

"Tomorrow. I can start as early as tomorrow if you need me to."

She walks away from the tortilla stand, and I assume she expects me to follow her.

"Let's do a quick interview," she nods toward the back of the kitchen.

I get four stare-downs from the cooks on the line; I'm a newbie on their turf. The kitchen is loud. Someone's dumping ice. Someone's banging a dirty dish against the garbage in an effort to get the cemented refried beans off the plate, and someone is hollering at a cook about an order gone bad.

We make our way through the kitchen, and the slim and trim manager (how's she so skinny working around quesadillas?) unlocks her office door with a key that hangs from a key ring worn around her wrist.

"Excuse the mess," she says, but doesn't try to give reason as to why the place looks like a hoarder with a notebook fetish lives here. She clears a chair for me to sit in, and I take a seat and cross my legs.

It dawns on her that she hasn't introduced herself, so she turns around and says, "I'm Angela," and offers her hand. I shake it and get the sense that she's beyond exhausted. Dark circles. Haphazard makeup. Last night's hairdo.

Three questions later, I'm hired.

On the drive home I think about the worker at the Goodwill.

Contentment.

Chapter 42

Dad's upbeat mood from the morning has petered out. When I walk through the door, he's on the couch flipping through the channels.

"Hey, Dad. How'd it go?" I feel like a parent asking their child about the first day of school.

He continues to flip channels. "Aw, it was alright. It's a job." His enthusiasm is lacking.

"Well, guess what?" I begin enthusiastically, trying to change the energy.

"What?" Dad says.

I plop down beside him.

"I got a job too."

This news causes him to actually look in my direction.

"You did? Where?"

"At the Mexican restaurant down the street. I guess they're in desperate need of help because the manager told me I could start hostess training tomorrow."

"Well honey, that's great. We'll be rolling in it before too long with two paychecks coming in."

Reality check.

"I don't think we'll be rolling in it, but hopefully we can get caught up on some bills soon."

He stares at me. For an uncomfortable amount of time.

"I'm really proud of you," he says.

What? Did he really just say he was proud of me?

"Thanks, Dad." I force the words from my mouth. "I'm proud of you too, Dad."

◆

Three weeks later, my boss hands me my first paycheck, and I look for the printed numbers immediately. $214.36.

I'm ecstatic, to say the least.

I go straight to the bank to cash it. Although it's money already spent, it feels so nice, these two $100 bills in my hands. It triggers the memories of a big win, and the rush of having stacks of money in my purse. It's the equivalent of an alcoholic taking that one little sip. The one little, dangerous sip that sends everything spiraling.

Then, even though I shouldn't, I do it.

I go to the library.

I Google it.

I find it.

I make a plan in my head, but push it back out and make the thought go away.

That night, I can't sleep. I try deep-breathing. I flip my pillow to the cold side a million times. I stare at the clock in disbelief that it's one thirty in the morning, and I haven't fallen asleep yet.

I drink a glass of milk.
I rub my own shoulders.
I count sheep.
I think about my new job.
Nothing's working.
I give up.
I put on a baseball cap and tiptoe through the house.

And some time later, at two o'clock in the morning, I find myself walking into a new, different casino.

Looking for something.

ABOUT THE AUTHOR

Julie Dill lives in Oklahoma City where the wind always comes sweeping down the plains—literally.

As a young girl she always wanted to be a teacher, so she went on to receive her Bachelor of Science in Education degree from the University of Central Oklahoma and taught in elementary schools for ten years. Currently, she serves as an adjunct professor and loves helping students achieve success. One of her greatest professional accomplishments is earning her National Board Certification.

She holds a Master's of Fine Arts in Creative Writing from Oklahoma City University and continues to work on various writing projects. From hiking in Colorado, to playing poker in Vegas, she's always up for a new challenge. Julie is a busy mom of two teenage daughters, and any extra time that she may carve out is spent reading, writing, and rooting for the Oklahoma City Thunder.